MORGUE DRAWER FOUR

Forthcoming by Jutta Profijt:
Morgue Drawer Next Door
Morgue Drawer for Rent
Dirt Angels

MORGUE DRAWER FOUR

Jutta Profijt

TRANSLATED BY Erik J. Macki

amazoncrossing

Morgue Drawer Four by Jutta Profijt was first published in 2009 by Deutscher Taschenbuch Verlag GmbH & Co. KG in Munich, Germany, as *Kühlfach 4*.

Translated from the German by Erik J. Macki.
First published in English in 2011 by AmazonCrossing.

Published by AmazonCrossing
P.O. Box 400818
Las Vegas, NV 89140

ISBN-13: 978-1611090321
ISBN-10: 1611090326
Library of Congress Control Number: 2011901818

PROLOGUE

I hope you'll read this account from top to bottom because it's the whole truth and nothing but the truth, and so on— eh, I'm sure you've heard the saying. Personally, I couldn't care less what you're going to think about the things that have transpired over the past two weeks, but it's important to my friend Martin that ultimately you're able to see all the crap people have been saying about him for what it is: a festering pile of allegations and rash pop-psych analyses (or, dumbass psychobabble—honestly, I'd normally have written "psycho shit," but Martin is a champion of elevated diction, so I've been trying to make an effort). He and I are about as different as two people can be. Like fire and water, heaven and earth. You'll grasp the deeper sense of the latter simile later on, so just keep reading, *¡ándale, ándale!*

What I'm trying to do here is restore the reputation of my friend, Martin Gänsewein. He's the only friend I've got, and—because of the special circumstances of my current existence—the only friend I'm ever likely to have.

ONE

The day everything began—as I now know—started out horribly, which is to say rock-bottom, and I should've taken that as a warning. But, and in my own defense I've got to say, that's how most days used to start. In other words, never before noon, a disgusting taste in my mouth, a thick, furry otter's pelt on my tongue, construction workers in a race to pound the most nails into my head, and the usual craving for a cigarette, a beer, and a girl.

There wasn't any beer around, I'd actually have had to stand up to get a cigarette, and I hadn't gotten laid for a pretty long time. As I lay there semicomatose for a little while, it suddenly occurred to me: I was frigging late. Most days that wasn't a problem, but on this day I had an important appointment. A job. An important job for an important man. I'd really wanted to do everything right, and now I'd overslept! I guess I was lucky that the pressure building up in my tailpipe interrupted my peaceful slumber. Of course, if Martin were here now he'd say it wasn't the pressure in my "tailpipe" but in my "bladder," since Martin likes being so precise. But at the time I didn't know him yet at all. I would get to know him only a few days later under circumstances that were for me distinctly unpleasant, which is why my wording for biological imperatives was still pretty amateurish and, I now see, imprecise.

If I had suspected that this day would determine the course of the rest of my life, I'd obviously have stayed in bed. But I had no idea, and even looking back I can't see any signs that might have portended the impending disaster. So I got up and headed toward my demise just as blindly as I was shuffling into the bathroom.

Normally I don't risk looking into the mirror at this hour, but since I had something planned I eventually subjected my appearance to a critical review. Now, I wouldn't want you think that I used to express myself in words such as "critical" and "review" right out of bed; I've added these words to my active vocabulary only because of Martin. I actually don't think about much at all right before a shower, and if I do, it's only monosyllabic grunting and grumbling.

So, I spent a while trying to blink open my eyes that were glued shut with sleep until I could make out where the mirror was hanging, but then I suffered a mild shock as the visage staring back at me came into focus.

As the image sharpened, my recollection of Bennie's new knife returned. He'd been brandishing the thing, looking for something to slice up and demonstrate how sharp the blade was. His hunting eyes landed—on me. I was standing within reach, and he grabbed my hair with his left hand and gave me a new haircut in a lightning strike. Because I flinched—and only because of that, as Bennie later emphasized—the blade also slit open my left eyebrow as he finished my haircut. So a thin stripe of dried blood trailed down the face in the mirror, from eyebrow to chin, and realizing this hideous countenance was in fact my own, I totally freaked out.

I splashed a good deal of warm water on myself until I looked somewhat civilized again, although I had spent the past five years trying to shed just this kind of civilization that was the result of growing up in my parents' home. But my important job required an inconspicuous appearance, and so after showering I picked out jeans, a dark jacket, and a wool cap that hid the results of the knife incident on my head pretty well. A final review in the dusty mirror on my wobbly wardrobe revealed the image that I had made such an effort to achieve: a medium-height, inconspicuous, somewhat spindly fellow with longish hair that I had pulled up under my cap. Nondescript appearance, dishwater blond, straight nose, weak chin, and slouchy shoulders. A Joe Schmo even the most curious witnesses wouldn't be able to give a specific description of. And that's how I wanted to look, because somehow I thought that that would help me. What total bullshit!

———•———

I hoofed down to the parking lot in front of the "Cologne Congress Centre," which is just the fancy name for the convention center downtown. If you're standing in the right spot, you can just make out the illuminated spires of Cologne Cathedral and Great St. Martin Church, right across the Rhine from there.

Now, if you want to steal a car, it's not advisable to drive your own car there and then take off in the stolen car. The cops aren't as stupid as a lot of people think. They're pretty quick to check out all the cars parked near the scene of the crime, and then they'll nab you faster than you can turn around. So keep that in mind; it's good advice from an expert.

Public transportation is totally the pits. That's why I went on foot, walking my toes down to stumps and slowly growing blisters on my heels because I'm not the strolling-around type. I mean, what else would God have invented cars for, then? I finally made it to the aforesaid parking lot, and it was in fact full of some of the coolest rides that those yodeling autoworkers in Stuttgart or Munich or wherever bolt together in their fancy high-tech factories. Each with more horsepower than the next—lower, faster, hotter. Special trims, limited editions, and custom jobs to the customers' specifications. Fifty wet dreams all in one semi-public parking lot without any surveillance to speak of. A parking lot distinguished not by its security but by its proximity to the main entrance. A lot where only VIP visitors can park. A lot with only one single camera covering several hundred square meters, one key cabinet that any nitwit could pry open with their mom's SuperFitness ID card: i.e., a typical German security disaster. No awareness of the problem even though more than fifty thousand cars are stolen every year in Germany. Before they came out with electronic immobilizers, incidentally, it was twice that. And I rank among those who can handle even the tricky cases.

So in the dimming twilight I walked as inconspicuously as possible at an inconspicuous gait in my inconspicuous outfit through the parking lot, and I took a look around—inconspicuously, of course. And there she was. Until that moment I had never believed there really were people so totally and abysmally stupid. People who would leave a Mercedes-Benz SLR McLaren in an unmonitored parking lot in front of a convention center, imagining their car will still be there to stroll back to after wrapping up their Mr. Important-Convention-Attendee routine so they can climb into their half-million-euro boat and cruise home to Mommy. But sure enough, there she was, sitting amid the smoking Daimlers, Jags, BMWs, and even a Bentley—the SLR that my client had told me about. Olli wanted it.

———•———

Olli's a car smuggler. Of course he's not listed in the Yellow Pages under "Car Smugglers." He's listed under "Car Repair, Purchase, and Sales," and basically that's pretty accurate, too. Only he sells way more cars than he buys because his procurement system proceeds largely without sales contracts and other pesky paperwork. Olli is a really big operator with contacts in Eastern Europe. I'm sure you're thinking Russia or Poland, but that's not where his customers are. Nowadays any old cleaning lady is doing business with Russians and Poles; they're so mainstream now they've become white-bread again. Olli does business with a crew from one of those tiny countries; I'm not that good with that corner of the map, I don't recall the name.

Doesn't matter. Anyways, Olli knows the whole north-south-east-west car smuggling scene like his own back pocket. He knows me pretty well, too; I used to work for him off and on until we had a stupid run-in with each other this one time because of this thing. Normally it'd be way beneath him to ever take notice of my existence again, but last night he sent one of his tools over to my place. He gave me the job that I was in the middle of executing right now.

———•———

I don't want to give away any details, since stealing an SLR is a delicate matter, and I'm kind of proud of being one of the few guys who has the necessary tricks and talents. So that's why I won't pass them on, even though, unfortunately, this knowledge isn't going to be of any use to me anymore. But to make a long story short: I stole the ride from the parking lot. Unfortunately because of my good night's sleep and long walk into town, this happened somewhat later than planned, so the fat cats whose wheels were parked in the lot were already marching back out into the lot like tin soldiers in three-piece uniforms right as I started the engine. Now, the sound that an SLR makes cannot be confused with that of pretty much any other car, which is to say that about fifty sets of eyes turned my way as I raced the car out of the lot. In my rearview mirror I could just make out the hint of a wave, like in a stadium, as forty-nine arms pointed in my direction and one hand sank into the front pocket of a suit jacket, presumably to extricate a cell phone and call the cops. But then I lost interest in the scene behind me, focusing on driving my new acquisition fast, but not too fast, through the dark streets of downtown Cologne toward the entrance to the autobahn. During evening rush hour in winter when it's dark, with freezing drizzle, even a semi can vanish into the thick of things faster than someone who can't swim vanishes over Niagara Falls, and in that moment I had good reason to think my heist had gone OK.

I resisted the urge to drive too fast, tailgate other drivers, pass on the right, change lanes at the last moment before turning, and all of the other urges that make driving a car so supersonically awesome, because I did not want to catch anybody's attention. If you're sitting in a stolen car, you should drive more properly than you would even for your driver's test. I kept at it. I was going to need twenty-seven minutes to make the agreed rendezvous, and I made it with forty-five seconds to spare. Shit! I could have used another couple of minutes, because before you hand off a stolen car you've got to empty it out. You've got to dig everything that you can make use of or sell out of the glove compartment, all the storage cubbies and pockets, the trunk, and under the seats. So now I needed to do a turbo pass through the car. Glove compartment: maps, condoms, sunglasses, a set of pens. Under the seats: a wad of cash, couldn't count it at a glance, no matter, grabbed it. In the trunk: a naked woman.

I slammed the trunk back shut, hyperventilated a bit, opened the trunk again, and looked at her lying there. Half on her back, her knees fully bent, her arms at her sides, her body turned a bit. She was small and delicate, but she totally filled the tiny trunk. I nudged her with my finger; she was ice cold. I pushed one of her arms a bit to the side and jumped when I saw how the underside of her arm was purple. I pressed a finger to the spot where I thought her carotid was: nothing. She had tattoos around her ankles, she was quite pretty even though her makeup was on too thick, and she was dead as a tire iron. I shut the trunk back over her, carefully, as though she might have minded if I slammed it with a loud bang. Then I leaned on the driver's side door, fumbled a cigarette out of my jacket, lit it, and sucked so deeply that I smoked half the cigarette in one breath.

I had to ditch it. The body, not the cigarette. You don't hand a car smuggler a car with a corpse in the trunk, not even if it's an SLR. Or all the less if it's an SLR? I was confused, but I knew the woman had to disappear. It's not like she was going to do it for me, so it was time for me to come up with a really clever solution for this highly unusual problem, and fast. I took one more deep drag, flicked the butt away, and was just about to get back into the car when I felt a hand on my shoulder. I flinched so much I hit my chin on the top of the car.

"Hey, Pascha, you're on time. Good job."

The guy grabbing me and praising me like some lame-ass nursery school teacher was Kevin, and he had a goatee that looked like his girlfriend had painted it onto his jaw with fine eyeliner, and he was always smirking. Maybe he suffered from Bell's palsy. But in any case I always found him repulsive, especially right now. He held out his palm.

I was gasping for air and howling because I hadn't just hit my chin but also bitten my tongue, and I was frantically running through my options for making the body in the trunk disappear before Kevin took the ride to Olli. It was no use, my brain was a crashed hard drive, and so, totally exhausted, I just dropped the keys into Kevin's hand, and he said his buddy could drive me back into town. I stood there motionless in the parking lot for a solid five minutes until I could bring myself to puke the remains of my greasy midnight burger into the bowl of a rest-stop toilet. Then I felt a bit better, and I made my way home.

———•———

It would definitely have to be public transit this time, and I thought about what would probably happen next. Kevin had several hundred horsepower under his ass and would crash, and the car would catch fire, rendering both Kevin and the dead woman into fine ash. That was my favorite vision. But there was another. Kevin drove straight to Olli, who glanced into the trunk, got annoyed that I had served him up a mummy on the side that he had not ordered, and immediately dumped the body at the front door to my building. Or he would distribute leaflets with a photo of the dead woman with the words: "Are you looking for this woman? Ask Pascha, Telephone 022 . . ." Most likely, however, was that either Kevin or Olli would discover the body in the trunk, drive down the closest forest road, unload her there, and then sell the car to the East, just as planned. After all, I hadn't seen any pools of blood or other contaminants in the trunk, so the transaction involving the almost brand-spanking-new SLR could go off without a hitch.

Having arrived at this reassuring thought, I got out of the overcrowded bus and walked the short distance to my favorite gambling joint and slid a few coins into the slots. Slowly I started breathing normally again, although my tongue still hurt like hell when hot coffee with four spoons of sugar flowed over it.

I played for five hours until I didn't have a cent left. Not just all of my money, including the five hundred smackers out of the SLR, but worse: I owed Mehmet, the guy who runs the gambling joint, for several out-of-pocket loans, so my total debt at the end of the day ran a cool nineteen hundred euros. Not just debt from the slots, but that must already be obvious to you brainiacs. Mehmet was furious because officially he wasn't allowed to give out loans, and now he'd have to pay up for the loss himself. I kept on telling him about my big job, and I promised I'd bring him the cash as soon as

I got my cut. I hoped I would in fact get the dough Olli had promised me. My honeymoon would last forty-eight hours, and then Mehmet would hunt me down. The day had started out crappy, it had a catastrophic climax, and it had now ended in disaster.

———•———

I didn't hear a thing from Kevin or Olli the next day, or the next, and that was slowly making me nervous. The forty-eight hours that Mehmet had given me were soon over, and I didn't know how I was going to pay him back. I found fifty euros in my apartment, my emergency reserve in my rolled-up athletic socks that I hadn't worn for decades, but if I gave Mehmet my sock money I'd be totally broke and he'd still be angry, so that wasn't any solution. I started sitting around, alternately at home and at my favorite pubs, waiting for Kevin or another of Olli's errand boys to show up and give me the promised two thousand euros, and I was getting nervous as Mehmet's deadline approached. Even more nervous than I was before, I mean. I didn't want to be standing around all stupid like a cow at the slaughterhouse waiting for the guy with the bolt gun, so I took a seat in the first-available streetcar and just rode, changed lines, and directions, and rode back, transferred to the bus, and rode all over town. I transferred back to the streetcar, where it was alternately ice cold and screaming hot, and I managed to wangle a window seat and wipe the condensation from the pane; outside there were already two centimeters of snow. Perfect. I hate snow. Anyone who loves cars must hate snow.

I got off at a plaza with lots of people and a news kiosk, invested my sock money in alcoholic beverages, and took a train back downtown. I started getting tanked while I was still on the train. I got off somewhere—naturally I had the great fortune of landing in the middle of a roadwork site. And here I didn't think we were still investing in infrastructure in this country anymore. I climbed up some temporary stairs along with other riders, elbowing my way through the congestion points, then I got lost and at some point took a pedestrian overpass bridge labeled with a sign saying "All Downtown Lines: Straight Ahead." Meanwhile my field of vision had dramatically narrowed, the noises from my surroundings reached my jug ears as though from a great distance, but at least I wasn't all that worried about my debts.

I felt the impact on my back despite my drunken stupor. It caught me at the least opportune moment. In front of me there were two landings of stairs leading downward, with temporary railings. My foot reached out a bit farther than planned because of the impact, causing me to miss the first step. The second step was covered with snow and was thus slippery, so my worn sole slid over the edge. The thin board that was supposed to serve as a railing had about as much hold as a tow rope made of elastic. The nail that was supposed to connect the temporary railing to the support column on the left gave way immediately and without hesitation, and the nail on the right followed shortly thereafter. In those seconds my gift of observation was indescribably good, good as never before, and perhaps that alone should have given me pause, but I had no time for that. My feet slid forward through the railing, I tipped backward, and the back of my head hit the wood forming the surface of the bridge unbelievably hard before I completely sailed over the side. I experienced my plummet into the depths in slow motion. Spinning around some kind of axis I slammed onto the pavement six meters below. The noise that my body and above all my cranium made on impact startled even those who couldn't have seen my plummet at all because their backs were to me. As I was lying on my stomach with my face to the side, I was still able to make out faces turning toward me, but then I couldn't see anything anymore.

The darkness lasted for just a short moment, and then suddenly, I suppose after about ten seconds, I was able to observe the entire scene very clearly—from above. Now, I'm sure we've all seen our fill of those near-death-experience ghouls who haunt talk show after talk show, describing their mystic experiences. They all observe their bodies from the outside, and then comes the tunnel, and the light, blah blah blah. So I didn't give it much thought as I was floating over my twisted outer shell, which was littering the ground. I waited for the tunnel, the light, and ultimately to grow up again inside my own body. That's how those reborn TV freaks always end up describing it.

So I hung around and waited. I watched people giving my body a poke, someone taking charge and blathering something about calling for an ambulance, someone pressing on my wrist and carotid and with a serious face taking the cell phone from the man calling the police, reporting into it that the accident victim was dead.

Now wait just a second, I thought, that guy is totally exaggerating. He's welcome to pretend like he's in charge if he thinks he'll impress women that way, but there have got to be limits, thank you very much. Plus, his theatrical performance wasn't even resulting in the fairer sex throwing themselves at him, sobbing. The bystanders were just doing what bystanders do: standing around and staring.

———•———

I don't want to bore you with all the details, so I'll give you just the digest version of the most important things: the police came, determined that I had fallen off the makeshift pedestrian overpass, pronounced me—as I still thought, inaccurately—dead, and called the coroner's office.

"Hi, Rolf," said the short, chubby man in a dark brown duffle coat (really, I swear, he came in a duffle coat) to the uniform, as he set down his bag and checked my body for life signs. "Hi, Martin," Rolf, the policeman, replied.

"How long has he been here?" Duffie asked the crowd of gawkers who were now stamping their freezing feet behind the red and white cordon that had since been strung up.

"Seventeen minutes," answered the eager hero with paramedic training. Brownnoser.

"Accident or foul play?" Duffie asked.

"Unclear," replied a guy in civilian clothes who had given the orders for where the red and white tape should be strung up, and who generally gave the impression of being the guy calling the shots.

Policemen were scurrying around taking a thousand pictures of me, the bridge, the railing, and the bottle that had fallen out of my hand. They retraced the way I had come, measuring distances and angles, and they all looked terribly busy. Duffie—that is, Martin—knelt down next to me in the softly falling snow, studying me top to bottom, part of it actually through a magnifying glass he had pulled out of his bag. He combed every centimeter of my head, paying particularly close attention to the spot on the back of my head that had hit the plank on the wood overpass bridge, and then he crawled around with his face nearly to the ground trying to see as much as possible of the left half of my face, which I was lying on, before he finally turned me over. Then he did his examination again on my now-visible front side with the magnifying glass, and finally, finally he was through. He put the magnifying glass back into his bag, scanned around him, discovered what he was looking for, and gestured with his left hand. Two men came over, stuffed my body into my to-go box, and hauled me away.

———•———

As you can well imagine, I was totally freaked out. Those near-death-experience talk show attention-seekers on TV never mentioned the whole thing taking so long. They never said a word about people coming, recording your death, coroners staring at you like an insect under a magnifying glass, getting plopped into a box and hauled off.

Hauled off—*where to?* I suddenly wondered, feeling panic take over. How the hell am I supposed to find my way back into my body if I don't know where it is? You can imagine my horror. So I whooshed over behind the two figures who had just loaded the casket containing my body into a vehicle. Fortunately, and unlike the pallbearers, I did not slip on the icy street; instead I just whooshed through the air and flashed into the vehicle. Perhaps this as well should have given me pause, but we've already addressed this topic. I didn't have any time for pauses. I was just happy that I was still with my body as the vehicle started.

I didn't look out the window; I wasn't particularly interested where they were taking me so long as I was just with my body. At some point they went down a ramp, and then the vehicle's door opened; a long corridor was waiting for us, and then a door. They pulled open a stainless steel drawer and set my body inside; I wafted in afterward, of course, and then the drawer closed—and we lay in the dark, my body and I.

———————

Again, because of my confusion, and maybe as a side effect of the alcohol—I really didn't know if you could be wasted as a ghost having a near-death experience—I lacked any sense of time, but at some point the drawer opened, my body was placed onto a gurney, pushed into a tiled room, and transferred onto a stainless-steel table with an outlet strainer at the foot end, and then Duffie/Martin stepped up to the table along with another man. The other man was holding a Dictaphone and spoke the introduction into it. "Autopsy of a male body for the Cologne District Attorney's Office. Identified by the police as Sascha Lerchenberg, age: twenty-four, height: one hundred seventy-three centimeters, weight: sixty-nine kilograms."

I was still pretty confused, but that was entirely appropriate because what ensued was truly horrific. My initial confusion blossomed into full-on panic as I saw what Martin was holding in his hand: a gleaming scalpel that looked pretty damn sharp. He put it into position and sliced my entire torso open, starting at my chin in a straight incision going so far down you really couldn't go any farther. I expected a torrent of blood, but nothing happened. Meanwhile,

Mr. Blabbermouth commented into his stupid recorder on each incision and every finding while I circled above the autopsy table in extreme agitation. I felt sick. Layer by layer my skin was peeled off, the fat tissue underneath exposed and folded back—I don't remember all the details very well anymore—until the situation started to get really disgusting: Martin grabbed my testicles.

"Dude, get your monkey beaters off my balls!" I roared with the greatest urgency, and Martin spun around, so startled I thought he might slash his colleague right open. That was the moment I realized he could hear me.

TWO

"What is it?" the guy with the Dictaphone asked. I couldn't make out his whole face because slicer guys wear these ridiculous face masks when they're dissecting bodies, but his eyes had grown a little bigger out of fear as Martin's scalpel hissed through the air in front of his abdomen.

"I, uh, I don't know," Martin stammered, and I sensed his uncertainty. Ditto on that, plus I felt really indignant (that's another cool word Martin's taught me), I'm sure you can imagine. I mean, what would you say if some perv in green scrubs started by professionally filleting you and then wanted to cut your balls off? That's what I'm talking about.

"Do we need to prepare the testicles?" Martin asked, sounding somehow sheepish.

"Nah," came the response from behind the mask, the guy's eyes narrowing. He smirked big. "Only our female colleagues enjoy that. Leave them, it's OK. Cause of death is clear, right?"

Martin nodded. "Occipital blunt force trauma resulting in cardiopulmonary collapse due to massive brainstem injury, presumably the result of falling from the bridge onto the back of the head."

The other guy put the Dictaphone back up to his mask and said, "Preparation of testicles not necessary," then he switched it off and stretched. "Gotta pee."

Martin nodded. Martin stayed with me but took a step back from the table and watched his diminutive assistant, who was putting the pieces that Martin had cut out of my organs into Mason jars. At the time I wasn't able to make heads or tails of the scene, but since then I've learned that a fine tissue sample is taken from every organ, which in hospital slang is called a histo sample. Comes from *histology*, but you don't need to know that. Cutting the body open is only one part of an autopsy. There's also the toxicology report and even a genetic test, if they need one.

During my own autopsy, though, all I could do was circle around gawking, but otherwise I kept quiet. Martin was also unnaturally quiet. It was as though he were listening intently, uncertain whether he should be listening outwardly or inwardly. At first I left him alone.

The autopsy of my body was completed according to regulation and without further disruptions; the slaughterhouse—as I call the white-tiled room—was cleaned; and I— that is, the physical shell of me that had since been rather nastily disemboweled, restuffed with all the organs that had been taken out, and then sewed back up—was returned to my refrigerated drawer, labeled "Morgue Drawer 4." At the last moment before the drawer fully closed, I changed my mind, whooshed out of the narrow slit, and took position near the ceiling lamp where I had a good view of the room. There wasn't that much to see, because there wasn't anything to see apart from the refrigerated morgue drawers—inside which, incidentally, the prevailing temperature is four degrees Celsius. I hung out for a while wavering, then I made an attempt to get out into the corridor through the narrow crevice between the swinging doors. Bingo! Apparently quitting time had arrived down here because there wasn't a soul in the entire basement, which consisted of long corridors, the morgue and autopsy section, and a few storage rooms. Except for me, because I believe the term "soul" applies to no one as well as it does to me. I haunted (another word that had suddenly gained currency) around aimlessly and haphazardly. After spending quite a while like that, at some point I got bored, but I didn't trust myself to leave the basement, so I went back over in front of the door to my morgue drawer and daydreamed a little there in front of myself. At least I hadn't lost this skill, one I had always excelled in.

———

Again Martin was the first person I saw the next morning, and he exuded a distinctly palpable, nervous unease. Like when you're faced with a job you know is way over your head.

"Hi, Martin," I said, and from the terrified expression on his face I could see that he'd heard me again, or at least somehow sensed me, because when I write here that I "say" something, this of course has nothing to do with the production of sound waves, since for that one obviously needs vocal cords. Mine, however, were cut up into little pieces inside the dissected throat of the mincemeat corpse in Morgue Drawer Four.

"I'm Pascha, the guy in Morgue Drawer Four. You wanted to cut my balls off yesterday?"

Not the lowest-stress way to introduce myself, I admit, but at least it was direct and pertinent. He should know right away who he was dealing with.

"Sascha," Martin whispered. Of course he could have no way of knowing that I had changed the first letter of my name from S to P ever since that schlocky TV show with that guy named Sascha on it, and so now I go by Pascha. Nothing to do with Turkish brothels. I was nice enough to explain this to him.

Martin stood at the wall, his chubby face twitching and wriggling, its color resembling that of his chilled clients. He wiped his trembling hand nervously over his eyes.

"I'm hearing voices."

He didn't say that—he thought it, and I could hear it! Awesome!

"If you're hearing multiple voices, you should see the doctor, but if you're hearing just my voice, that's OK—after all, I've been talking with you the whole time!"

"Who are you?" he whispered.

"I just told you," I said, slightly annoyed. "I'm the guy who got pushed off that bridge; you examined me at the scene, and yesterday you practically puréed me on your table!"

"But you're dead; you can't speak to me," he objected.

All right, the man is a scientist, but still, for an academic I thought he was acting pretty stupid.

"Haven't you ever heard any of those near-death stories? You know, the soul leaves the body, hangs out for a while, and then at some point makes its way through the tunnel."

"Yes," he breathed.

"But there isn't any tunnel here; I don't know where I'm supposed to go."

He didn't say anything. I didn't say anything either, and so we each dwelled on our thoughts, with his forming a bewildered mess.

Suddenly the chaos of neurons within his brain reorganized itself, and a thought formulated itself clearly and distinctly out of the soup of letters: "You said you were pushed?"

"Duh," I said. "What, do you think I'd go and take a nosedive off a temporary bridge J4K?"

I couldn't literally see the question marks popping out of his gray matter, but the scientist was obviously unfamiliar with the truncated communication style of today's youth.

"You were severely inebriated," he objected, cautiously.

"Well, yeah . . ." I conceded. "I'd had a few . . ."

"Your blood alcohol level was three point seven," Martin countered; he likes to be precise, but I think I mentioned that already.

"Three point seven! Right on!" I was extremely impressed with myself. This pleasure did not persist, however, since my inebriated condition was apparently being used against me here. My murderer was going to get away with it because the official opinion was that my self-induced state of intoxication was the cause of my tumble from the bridge. That's just not what happened! And even worse, my buddies were going to think I was so wasted I died from my own stupidity. What kind of an obituary is that? "He was wasted and fell off a bridge!" So at that point, my vanity took over: the afterlife has to include a little bit of vindication, too.

"I was pushed," I emphasized, perhaps somewhat more expressively than was absolutely necessary, but in any case Martin rubbed his temples and groaned.

"All right," he moaned. "Please stop yelling at me that way."

"Take it easy," I said, making an effort to sound cool. "So tell me one more time exactly what the epitaph is that the cops are going to be carving onto my tombstone."

I felt those question marks popping up again like bubbles in the bathtub when you let one, but Martin had already understood more or less what I wanted from him.

"The police investigation didn't yield any suspicion of exogenous effect, nor did the autopsy. In view of the blood alcohol level, the snow on the stairs, and the poor condition of the railing, the cause of death was determined to be an accident resulting in fatality. However, there will also be an investigation because of the railing."

"That's bullshit," I said clearly and distinctly.

Martin winced.

"You've got to tell them that's not right," I demanded.

I considered this demand to be logical and quite simple. Pick up the phone, call the cops, let them know, done. But of course with academic types nothing is easy, let alone straightforward.

"On what basis should I make such an assertion?" Martin asked.

The question brought me precipitously close to the limit of my patience. Here he's got the ultimate witness to a murder, namely, the victim himself, and the doctor is asking on what basis he should disseminate the victim's knowledge of the details of the crime. Seriously?

"On the basis of my statement," I said, choosing my wording carefully and judiciously so as not to stoop to obscenities and insults, because I naturally wanted the good man to persist in his good will toward me. The problems you've got to put up with as a dead guy!

"That won't work," Martin objected. "No one will ever believe me." And after a short pause: "I don't believe it myself."

He rubbed his forehead again and passed his flat hand over his neatly trimmed haircut, a haircut that made him seem like one of those snooty do-gooders hosting some after-school special, and he hastily left the cold room. I let him keep his lead, strolling—if that's what you might call slowly gliding along without any hustle or bustle—behind him.

At first I kept close to Martin, using any doors that he opened so I could slip through myself, but that was pretty seriously slowing me down. So I started hanging back a bit, testing out my maneuverability. I could get through the narrowest crack in a door without any problem, and I could even whoosh through a keyhole. I brushed up along the ceiling, right over the floor, and even behind cabinets, and I determined that the only interesting vantage point is from above. You don't see much from behind a cabinet.

I grew braver and left the basement. In the stairwell I floated up one story step by step, but then I created my own sort of elevator by no longer zigzagging up the stairs but just shooting up vertically straight to the top through the center of the stairwell. When that got too boring, I entered the top floor and looked around there. That level—like the rest of the building, but at that point I of course didn't know this— was also full of offices and laboratories. Men and women, many of them in their let's-play-doctor coats, were sitting at lab tables and writing desks, standing in break rooms or crouched in front of whatever random equipment there was. They were acting like normal people—talking, making phone calls, drinking coffee and tea out of these unspeakably huge mugs the size of swine troughs with random witty quotes, horoscopes, or pictures of their babies on them. In other words, typical German office culture that, should a UFO occupation force land here one day, will prompt them to completely annihilate the human race. And we won't be able to blame those ooze-ridden creatures from outer space one bit!

Most of these folks, apart from their stupid mugs and lab coats, looked like totally normal people. So it wouldn't necessarily have occurred to anyone that all of them were spending their days slicing open bodies to remove their hearts, livers, kidneys, and other accessories and have a look-see at what the deceased had most recently eaten and when they had last screwed and whether there might somewhere be some kind of clue that Grandma didn't kick it from advanced age but rather had met her demise at the hands of a son, son-in-law, grandson, or the director of nursing services who was hoping to come into a fat inheritance soon. Now that's fucked up.

So far I had been crawling through the narrowest of crevices, but now I was ready to find out for sure: I assumed position in front of a wall separating two offices, concentrated, and—flashed through. Just like that. I didn't even feel like I had to rearrange my hair. Of course, I didn't have hair anymore, but you understand what I'm trying to say, right? I took the same way back through, and the only thing that was unpleasant about it was the visual perception. In other words: "What do you see?" And that's exactly the problem: "Nada." To be precise, I can't see what's behind a wall that I want to go through. So, it's like taking a running start, barrelling full steam ahead, and then you're already there. Where you may not even have wanted to go! It just felt somehow safer floating carefully through a door. It wasn't as abrupt.

I didn't feel like messing around by myself anymore, so I went in search of Martin, who I found in the break room. His cup was filled with weak tea, the little paper tag from the teabag hanging over the rim, mercifully concealing some motto by a Zen master printed on the cup's side.

Suddenly I wondered what cruel fate had bound me specifically to this man because—I had determined this immediately upon floating into the break room—I was receiving thought signals from no one else but Martin. I would really have preferred any type of signal at all from the other person present. It was a she, and bada bing. Long legs in well-worn jeans; tight turtleneck; wide, smiling lips; dark eyes; and a curly black mane she had casually tied back with a rubber band. Her white lab coat looked a little goofy, but no biggie—this was straight-up the Woman of My Dreams. Hanging out with chubby, Zen-tea-slurping Martin here in the break room. Didn't she have anything better to do?

Martin was actually managing not to constantly stare at her nicely shaped bazooms but look her in the eyes. How was he doing that? I searched his brain for the order printed in bold black capital letters: LOOK HER IN THE EYES! But there wasn't anything in there. He was just managing it. Was this guy queer?

"How was your weekend, Martin?" the fair maiden asked.

"Fantastic," Martin said. "And successful. I found four new maps."

"New new-maps, or new old-maps?" the Dream Woman asked.

"Old," Martin answered with a stupid grin.

What kind of garbage were these two blathering about? New old/new maps?!?

"And how was your weekend, Katrin?" Martin asked.

"Challenging," she replied, and I was about to start imagining what a challenging weekend with this woman looked like, but then she kept talking. "My brother and I had to clean out my parents' house, now that they've passed away."

"Doesn't she have a boyfriend?" I asked Martin.

Martin was in the middle of murmuring something that sounded like an apology and condolences, but my interim question threw him off. He hesitated mid-sentence and quickly took a sip from his mug.

"Push her down on her back," I challenged him. "A good screw will help her through her problems more than a bunch of crap condolences."

He snorted with a start into his tea, which slopped over the edge and ran down his sweater and pants.

Katrin reacted quickly, turning around to grab a towel. *All right!* I thought, into it. Now she was rubbing Martin's pants dry. He likely saw that coming, but instead of closing his eyes in pleasure and letting things run their course, he took the towel out of her hand and hectically tried to wipe his coat dry himself. How stupid can a guy be? An opportunity to get one rubbed out good by small, fast, feminine hands isn't something you pass up! What kind of issues had I stumbled across here, exactly?

"Aren't you feeling well?" Katrin asked.

The question had crossed my mind as well, although I had been thinking more about the mental and hormonal health of my fleshly friend, but she was surely asking because Martin's nose had gone pale and his cheeks were softly flushed, and he was acting all agitated.

"Yes, yes," Martin answered much too quickly. "I'm just fine, thank you."

Katrin didn't look convinced, and I couldn't blame her. It seemed like she wanted to say something else but thought better of it and said goodbye with a friendly, "See you this afternoon?"

Martin nodded.

"Have you no sense of decorum?" Martin hissed at me. And he really hissed it, even though thinking it would of course also have sufficed. "I would be truly grateful to you if you would refrain from interfering in my conversations."

I wanted to draw his attention to the fact that someone was standing in the door to the break room, but Martin kept on chewing me out.

"In particular I would like to request that there not be any dirty commentary or sexual innuendos from you when I'm speaking with female colleagues."

The man who was still standing in the doorway craned his neck forward a bit so he could get a view of the whole break room. Of course, he found no one in there apart from Martin.

"Hi, Martin. Everything OK?" the white lab coat asked as he walked in.

Martin spun around; now there was no further trace of paleness in his face—he was red as a lobster. "What? Oh, yes, yes, everything's just fine. How are things with you?"

The white lab coat nodded, stepped over to the coffee machine, glanced askance at Martin once more, and poured himself a mugful. Then something apparently occurred to him.

"Hey, did you catch the latest scoop on our favorite Bundestag representative, Dr. Christian Eilig?" he asked.

"No," Martin replied, sipping his tea.

"The paper has started calling him 'Dr. Christian' for short, and he wants to ban autopsies now."

"You're joking," Martin stammered, speechless.

"Unfortunately not," Martin's colleague said. "He says it violates the 'dignity of the human body' to cut it open."

Well, I could see where that guy was coming from, actually, but how did *he* know anything about it? Did they have Bundestag representatives who were dead, too? I wondered. And if so, how'd that bastard get back into his body?

Martin shook his head; whether out of aversion to the notions of their favorite Bundestag representative or just to shake himself free from my thoughts, I couldn't tell. "Didn't we have this debate already?" Martin asked. "About a thousand years ago?"

"Well, it's a hot topic again," his colleague said. "The TCP has been hitting seventeen percent in the latest polls."

"The 'True Christian Party,'" Martin muttered. "Ugh, how did we get stuck with a Bundestag representative like that?"

"Because the wise voters in Cologne elected him," his colleague replied. "Cologne Cathedral is apparently more important to them than forensic medicine."

"That man should stick to collecting all his high-end cars and let respectable people do their jobs," Martin grumbled.

His colleague nodded, patted Martin on the shoulder, picked his coffee mug back up, and left the break room.

Martin dumped the rest of his tea out into the sink and stormed in long strides down the hallway and into the stairwell, skipping every other step down, and finally arriving slightly out of breath in the morgue's refrigerated storage area. He pulled out Drawer Number Four and stared at me—or more precisely, at my body.

"How is that you're not dead?" he asked the body, which looked so dead it couldn't possibly look deader. Especially because of the really roughly resutured seam extending from my chin to my—well, you already know. His intonation was somehow irritated, and I didn't like the sound of it one bit. First of all, in contrast to the assertion he had just made, I was indeed quite dead; to that extent Meticulous Martin was mistaken—plus, I was the one who was in the really shitty situation here and not him. So if anyone should be irritated, clearly it should be me.

"Fuck you," I snarled at him. "I'm dead and no one knows that better than you; after all you're the one who sliced me clean open from top to bottom, ripped out every organ in my body individually, and then stuffed them all back inside, and you sewed me together so inelegantly that Dr. Frankenstein himself would be embarrassed about that suture."

By the time I finished talking, Martin was leaning against the morgue drawers next to mine; his legs were shaking so badly he could hardly stand. "But you're talking to me," he objected.

"Yeah, because it's pretty boring being all alone without any entertainment," I replied, although I knew very well what he was getting at. But I didn't have an explanation, either. I didn't remember missing a turnoff at any point. I hadn't been given any choice between moldering around here or hopping into a conga line with some procession of cherubim to convey me to the Pearly Gates, where Saint Peter would fling them open and ask if I've been a good boy.

How was I supposed to answer? Anyway, I didn't know why I was hanging out around here, myself, and I didn't know where all the other souls were, either. If they were anywhere at all. An old souls' home, a haunted house, some kind of heavenly Halloween hotel. So I couldn't explain anything to renowned no-clue-ologist Dr. Martin here, either; too bad for him.

"Do you believe in God?" Martin asked.

"Which one?" I asked, because I had gotten into the habit of giving that answer at some point, and I still thought it was clever. Plus, I haven't seen any cause to change it, for the reasons I've already given you. If there is some kind of chief overlord for the whole ball of wax, he had not introduced himself to me yet, in any case.

Although Martin had stopped talking, his thoughts were slowly ordering themselves into a serious bit of reflection. How, he was wondering, can I get rid of this guy? The question was entirely justified. Imagine being surrounded every day by about thirty corpses. That's your job, and you've gotten used to it. Well, it's actually not that bad, because at least dead people don't talk your ears off with whatever petty complaints, the way living patients do to their doctors. So things are actually pretty easy. Until the day a body suddenly shows up that's not quite as dead as it's supposed to be. For a scientist, that must surely be a terrible ordeal in and of itself, but the proposition that this errant soul may be just the beginning of some brand-new trend could make even one of your more-inured guys like Martin break out in a cold sweat. A vision of legions of specters swirling around him flashed through Martin's brain briefly, and he actually started trembling.

Of course now, in hindsight, I recognize that Martin's anxiety at that point was justified. He was just overwhelmed with the situation, and it's quite natural to wonder how to get rid of a ghost you didn't even summon. At that moment, however, as we stood in sweet communion before my refrigerated morgue drawer, I found what he was reflecting on nothing but revolting. I was dead, I had a problem, and he was wondering what the easiest way was to get rid of me again. Disgusting, right?

"Do you believe that your soul will be able to find peace if we solve your murder?" he said, wording his question carefully.

Ha! Did he really think the wool can so easily be pulled over my eyes? Whether or not my soul found peace was totally beside the point for him. What he wanted was for my soul to disappear—no matter, heaven or hell, as long as I was gone. That's how I felt at the time, at least.

"I think so," I said, because if he was hoping to get rid of me again by solving the crime, then he would certainly make an effort to find my murderer and restore my reputation. My reputation as a person who was important enough for someone to kill. Who didn't plunge off the bridge out of sheer stupidity. A martyr, a war victim of Cologne's brutal underworld.

Martin sighed. "OK, then please recount the sequence of events for me, the backstory, everything you know."

Now I had a problem, because even if I really, really do like to go boozing now and again, three point seven is pretty high, even for me, and I had only hazy recollections of many of the details.

But I told Martin about my last day in as much detail as possible.

"You didn't see anyone at the station or on the over-pass?" Martin asked.

"Of course I saw people," I said. "But no one that I knew."

"And the person who pushed you, you didn't see them, either? Not even—" Martin hesitated. "Not even as you were falling?"

"You mean after I was already lying dead in the snow and my soul slowly started wafting up, I should have been able to get a good look at the murderer from that vantage?"

He nodded.

"Well," I replied after a moment's thought. "Maybe I did see him, but I didn't recognize him. You don't become all-knowing just because you're dead."

Too bad, Martin thought, and I had to agree with him on that. In general my condition was subject to considerable limitations. I was able to make contact with only one single human being, and although I could sense his thoughts, I wasn't able to speak out loud. Plus, I had to actually move from place to place, so I couldn't beam myself up or move objects around, either. I hadn't imagined it like this at all.

"Then we'll have to approach the issue in a different way," Martin said. He was no longer trembling, but he was still pale. "Who might have had reason to kill you?"

I should've expected that question to come up, but it threw me for a second, all the same.

Try it out yourself: At some quiet moment in your life, ask yourself who might feel like offing you. Well? Weird, right? So right off the bat obviously all the usual suspects occurred to me. My ex, who I played for a couple hundred smackers. Mehmet at the casino, who I owed money. Pablo, which isn't his real name, but that's the name I knew him by, he'd been my dealer before he landed in the pen—which he blamed me for! Of course, on lengthier reflection other names would occur to me, and of course it might also be possible that stealing the SLR with the body in the trunk might have resulted in a certain irritation when it reached its intended destination. The only question was, what destination. The owner of the car? Olli? His Eastern European buyer?

"My ex threatened many times, and in front of witnesses, to knock me off one day," I let drop, with forced casualness. "That bitch thinks I played her."

"Di-did you?" Martin asked, stammering out of nervousness.

"Well," I started slowly, immediately glinting into Martin's brain for the answer: he thought I did!

"Put the heat on her, then we'll see what turns up," I said. I was overcome by a certain joyous anticipation. I pictured grim, beautiful images in my head: a drill team of the boys in blue marching in unison up to Nina's door, knocking, dragging her out into the hall as soon as she opened the door, and then asking her the same question over and over again: "Why did you kill your ex-boyfriend?"

She would smoke until she didn't even have any butts left, the cops wouldn't let her out to get any new ones, and hour by hour she would have to answer the same question over and over again. Sweet.

"We can't involve the police," Martin explained.

"Why not?" I asked.

"Because the autopsy report didn't indicate any signs of foul play, and the police are also assuming it was an accident. The investigation into your death has been concluded."

"Then you have to open the case up again," I said.

"We've already discussed that issue," Martin countered. "I can't tell the police that the murder victim himself told me that he was killed."

"Then you have to talk to my ex," I said, but my excitement had already waned. Martin was a wuss. He'd politely ask Nina in his cautious way whether she might possibly have killed her ex-boyfriend, and she would ask him if his brains were in his ballsack. Then she'd get some idea into her head and start licking her tongue over her lips, wrapping a strand of hair around her finger, and looking around discreetly for the hidden camera. And when she realized there wasn't any camera, she'd glare at him like he was a rat with a boil at the base of his tail and then throw him out, plain and simple. Sayonara, O you beautiful third degree.

Martin took down Nina's name and address. He wanted to head over there after work today, and I decided not to warn him that obviously I intended to tag along.

The rest of the day passed without any incidents worth mentioning, if you disregard the fact that a suicide victim was delivered to determine the cause of death. Considering that a freight train loaded with new cars fresh off the line at one of Cologne's large auto plants had cleanly cut the man's body in two right above the navel, I couldn't really see any need for a detailed autopsy because I'd have guessed the cause of death as—surprise!—dismemberment, but Martin and his colleagues are resolute. A body that did not die from heart failure, old age, or some other natural cause is investigated very carefully, period.

I kind of kept out of the way during the autopsy; my own was still too fresh in my mind, and at the time the systematic dismantling of corpses still struck me as pretty repulsive. Over time I've overcome this timidity, but more on that later.

———•———

At quitting time Martin said goodbye to his colleagues. We didn't see Dream Woman again all day long, which I was very sorry about. The white coat who had surprised Martin in the break room while he was busy arguing with himself at the top of his voice took one more skeptical look at him, but he was apparently unable to see any further signs Martin was wrestling with demons. (Eh? Get it? Not bad, right? A sense for the nuance of language is another thing Martin has taught me, but I think I mentioned that already.) Martin hung his white office jacket properly onto a hanger, in contrast to his green slaughterhouse top, and left the "Institute for Forensic Medicine at the University Medical Center of the University of Cologne"—as the whole, cripplingly long title of this institution reads—then put on his duffle coat, and walked out to his . . . little trash can on wheels. You know, a Deux Chevaux, 2CV. Duck. Snail. Silver Hornet. Seriously, I'm not lying! He actually drives one of those swaying boxes that people hang up on ski lifts as cable cars or push on tracks through the haunted house ride at a carnival, which should be banned from driving on public streets, incidentally. You wouldn't go driving around your neighborhood on your lawnmower or bolt an auxiliary engine onto your five-wheeled, height-adjustable, lumbar-supporting office chair, thus rendering the whole downtown area unsafe, would you? All right then.

Anyways, we made our way in this ridiculous shoebox to the apartment of Nina, my ex. The necessity of commending my spirit to the most embarrassing vehicle since Fred Flintstone's Flintmobile convertible was an even greater humiliation than when my pediatric dentist discovered that I, unlike most people, was born without wisdom tooth buds. Fortunately—and this was the very first moment I really appreciated the immateriality my death had forced upon me—no one could see me sitting with Martin in this thing.

"Do you know what this vehicle was invented for?" I asked Martin as he turned the ignition.

I thought he had suffered a mild coronary, and it took me a while to get that he had not anticipated my presence and had not noticed me. He got the swaying box back under control before almost careening into a light pole, and he breathed deeply, in and out, several times.

"So, do you know?" I started the thread of the conversation again.

"To drive," he retorted. Ridiculous!

"To let your eggs swing free," I said, correcting him. "The specification when they were developing the 2CV said to build a car where eggs in a basket would remain unbroken even on a bad stretch of road. In those days, right after World War II, people still used to transport their eggs in baskets and not in cartons."

"Uh-huh," Martin said, but he didn't sound all that interested.

"Plus, even an untrained female driver was supposed to be able to handle it easily."

"Interesting," Martin mumbled.

"So . . ." I said, bringing my reflections to their logical conclusion, "what's up with the trash can car? You're not a chick, and you're not a chicken egg."

"I like the car, and it's economical."

Yes, liking it and economicality were of course very important considerations when choosing a set of wheels. Whereas criteria like engine performance, chassis design, coolness factor, or just that awesome sensation like you're letting a clear-coated Rottweiler off leash when your right foot just barely taps the gas—that's all just crazy. We like our cars, and they ought to be economical. People like Martin should ride bikes. Or better yet: tricycles.

Given that the Luddite sitting here next to me driving the automotive equivalent of a rotary phone was going to have to serve as the "extended arm" of my investigation, and given that my motivation to pursue said investigation was not inconsiderable, I didn't want to annoy him, so I discontinued the discussion of that topic.

———•———

I navigated Martin through rush-hour traffic and was admittedly pleased that he found a parking spot right in front of Nina's apartment. See, I was pretty scared of spending time out in the open. I felt like any gust of wind might sweep me up, blowing me several hundred meters or even kilometers away so I couldn't come back anymore. The idea was so haunting that I kept right up close to Martin's dweeby wool coat until we were standing on the front stoop of the apartment building. Martin called up, the intercom didn't work, but the door was buzzed open, and we entered the dirty entryway. In his coat, neatly combed hair, unfashionably comfortable leather shoes, and wide eyes, Martin looked as out of place as Queen Elizabeth under the purple neon lights in the public bathrooms at the train station. But what could I do? Plus, the surprise effect is always good when you want to ask dumb questions, and Nina would presumably totally lose it at the sight of this creature arisen from the slightly stuffy, unhip world of academia. Which she did, too, right on cue.

Martin introduced himself, said his name was Gänsewein ("goose wine"—seriously, that's his name! Apparently an old joking way of saying "water," like how the English say "Adam's ale"; I hadn't known that before, either, and I couldn't help snickering), and he had a few questions regarding my death. Martin nodded when she offered coffee, and plopped onto the battered old leather couch that I knew used to belong to the old man in the apartment next door. After a heart attack he was able to leave the apartment again only feet-first. That was the moment when Nina and my successor pinched the worn-out piece of furniture. And now she was proud as the winner of the Miss Suburban Cologne pageant for being able to call a piece of leather furniture of such exquisite quality her own. She made coffee for the man she addressed as "Doctor," which meant she plunged two tablespoons of the cheapest instant into a coffee mug, topped it with hot tap water, and stuck in a spoon she'd wiped off on the cuff of her sweatshirt. I myself used to prepare my own coffee with exactly this method, although I usually forwent measuring it with the spoon—so the swill was sometimes stronger and sometimes weaker, and I didn't think anything of it. But with Mannered Martin sitting on the stolen couch, suddenly this sort of coffee culture struck me as somehow deficient.

While Nina was going about her hostess activities, Martin and I had enough time to give the apartment a good look-see. I don't know whether death actually brings a person's spirit closer to something higher, but in any case coming back to this apartment—which had been like my second home for a while—was a confrontation with what is commonly known as a Vale of Tears.

The three ashtrays on the coffee table and the fourth on the windowsill were overflowing, and based on the distinct, browning tinge to the rugs and curtains, one could deduce that the enjoyment of tobacco wares was a full-time occupation in here. Of course, I already knew that from before, but I was never so aware of how acrid tobacco smoke can make a place. The two plants sitting on the windowsill could have worked as extras in one of those spaghetti westerns as withered tumbleweeds rolling in the wind across the dusty streets of a Mexican village. The only paper with words printed on it was the TV guide, which exhibited various marks from coffee cups and beer bottles. And the cushion on the stolen couch had that universal ass-shaped depression in it that you can see in any German living room.

Nina finished her coffee-serving ritual, accompanied as usual by a hastily swallowed "fuck" as she touched the mugs not on the handle but on the body, thereby ascertaining that the ceramic was indeed hot. I glanced into the kitchen and thanked providence that Martin could see only the living room, and I caught myself wondering what degree of civilization one could expect from someone whose kitchen is smaller than the guest bathroom at my parents' house.

Nina came over and sat across from Martin.

"Have you heard that Sascha Lerchenberg passed away?" he asked, and actually said "passed away."

"Yeah."

Just a one-word answer out of the mouth of a woman whose vital functions, unlike those of most people, didn't consist of inhaling and exhaling but of inhaling and chattering. I have never caught her just exhaling air. Words were always part of it; her whole body seemed to be filled with them, and they seemed just to pour out of her. Nina can jabber, blabber, blather, yap, drivel, gabble, prattle, ramble, and just about anything else that in some way has to do with speaking.

But here and now on her couch I wasn't getting the impression that Nina was unable to say more because she was overwhelmed with such great sorrow; instead, the reason for her uncharacteristic linguistic inhibition was something else. She looked irritated, and presumably she wasn't totally sure what reaction was expected from her, so she held back accordingly. She crossed her long legs in her shiny pink polyester track pants and tried to smile.

"Would you think it possible that he was murdered?"

What kind of a question is that supposed to be? Would you think it possible that ten million years ago dinosaurs lived on earth? No? Well, then, there must not have been any! I really wanted to pull out my hair, but as some kind of eviscerated ethereal entity this reaction was of course precluded. Martin, wake up! You're the cop, she's a suspect, put the screws on her!

Martin nervously wiped his hand over his forehead.

"Um, well, I don't know," was the poorly qualified answer from my dear ex-hag, but you can't in any seriousness expect a sensible answer to an idiotic question. I hastened to share this conclusion with Martin, and in response he grew even more nervous.

"Would you know anyone who might have any reason to kill him?" he asked.

"Pablo," Nina said without hesitating. "I don't know what his real name is, but Pablo thinks it's Sascha's fault he's in prison."

"But if Pablo is in prison, he can't have killed Sascha," Martin objected.

Nina shrugged, pouted, and thought. At least, she pretended to. Whether any actual activity takes place in her brain in a situation like this, I have never been able to ascertain.

"Why do you ask?" she suddenly wanted to know. "Sascha and I haven't been together for a couple of months."

Hopefully he doesn't answer now, I thought. If Martin were a cool guy in a cool movie, at this point he'd say, "I'm asking the questions here," but I didn't think Martin was capable of that. And I was right—he let the opportunity pass. Still, he didn't answer, either, but instead asked another question.

"Why aren't you together anymore?" he asked.

"Because he conned me." She literally spit the words.

"That's not true," I yelled before Martin could continue. "It wasn't like that."

"What happened?" Martin wanted to know from Nina, and we both starting talking at the same time.

"Not over each other," he yelled, irritated, and Nina gawked at him as though he'd suddenly put on a red and white cap and started singing "Jingle Bells."

"What do you mean 'over each other'?" she asked. She narrowed her eyes into slits; her expression was truly frightening. Provided, of course, that one could be frightened of a skirt.

"Pardon me; I meant, please start again," Martin stuttered. I forced myself to keep my trap shut because otherwise he'd totally screw up the questioning, which already seemed doomed.

"He was supposed to fix my car, but he wangled me out of the money because he said he had to buy replacement parts. The beater ran after that, but a week later it wouldn't start up again. So he took my money for parts again, and then it worked well for a week, but that was it. I asked a friend of mine to take a look at it, and he thought that there weren't any new replacement parts in it at all."

"And then?" Martin asked as Nina sucked on her cigarette butt, her anger heating up like a can of ravioli on the stove.

"So then he was supposed to sell the piece of junk for me, which he did, but then he told me he got only four hundred for it. Later on someone told me that was a lie, too; he'd actually gotten six hundred. So he stole two hundred euros from me, too."

I kept my mouth shut. Nina was wrong, but I didn't need to saddle Martin with that. I'd moved her car for a cool eight hundred. To a half-blind Turk who wanted to drive that bedpan on wheels back home to his brother-in-law in Anatolia. I suspect he didn't even get it across the Rhine, but since he didn't know my actual name, I didn't really care. Incidentally, I used the extra four hundred to settle my gambling debts—and, as we well know, gambling debts are debts of honor. So it was an honorable thing, the story with Nina's car.

"Would you have any reason to think that his death was connected with this, uh, auto sale?" Martin asked, and I was slowly but surely developing a deep disinclination toward questions that began with "Would you . . ."

"Uh-uh," Nina said, stubbing out her cigarette. "Why would anyone have waited so long? He conned me over the car months ago now."

"Well, then . . ." Martin mumbled, standing up. He had taken only two sips of his coffee, and he made no effort to finish the mug before he left. "Thank you very much," he added, briefly shaking Nina's hand, and walked out the door with his coat over his arm. I had to hurry to keep up.

———•———

"What did these enhanced interrogation techniques produce in terms of actionable information?" Martin asked in a tone that wavered between irritability and resignation once he was finally seated back inside his hamster wheel, having locked the world outside.

"It wasn't her," I said, because I had decided not to pepper him with criticism right away.

"How do you know that?"

"She can't lie. If she had pushed me, it'd have been all over her face."

Martin relaxed a little.

"I can't do this," he said.

Secretly I had to admit he was right, of course, but I needed him, so I sucked up to him a little. "Well, that was a pretty good start." Somehow at that moment I felt glad that I didn't have a face anymore because I couldn't have kept a straight face at such a bald-faced lie otherwise. Even I'm not that good.

"Best you jot down some notes," I suggested, because I didn't have any idea what the memory capacity of a disembodied corpse is. Martin nodded.

"And then take me back to the Institute," I added. Of course, I didn't feel like spending a boring night inside Morgue Drawer Four, but I was smart enough not to ask Martin for anything else tonight. And his reaction confirmed I was right. When the scope of my request really seeped into his brain, he quickly started nodding with such enthusiasm I was worried his head would shake right off his neck. The man urgently needed a break. He put the car into gear and drove to the Institute. As we were just stepping through the main entrance, a man walked up to us from inside, and it turned out this guy was Martin's best friend and a true-blue plainclothes.

"Hello, Gregor. Did you bring me some new work?" Martin asked, vigorously shaking his counterpart's hand.

"No, our attractive new colleague is on this one," Gregor answered. He gave a wide and, as I soon realized, slightly suggestive grin. "The lovely Katrin."

Ah ha! On mention of this name I sorely missed my erectile tissue as Martin recalled the embarrassing situation in the break room.

"She said you seemed a bit confused today," Gregor said, scrutinizing him.

"Well, of course," I interjected. "With a dream woman like that, the arrow always wants to hit its target, so there's nothing but white noise inside the skull."

Martin gave an answer along the same lines, content-wise at least, and Gregor scrutinized him even closer.

"Are you falling for Katrin's charms? Wow, that's a new one," he answered. "What about Birgit?"

"Birgit?" I echoed.

"Yes, uh, of course I'm actually not that interested in Katrin, but rather in Birgit, although you knew that already."

At the moment, unfortunately, Martin's articulacy (another word he taught me) left a lot to be desired. Gregor's face was growing more and more skeptical.

"Say," Martin began, "are there still any investigations open on that accident on the overpass bridge at the construction site? That man who fell off it?"

Gregor shook his head. "No evidence of foul play. Why? Isn't the autopsy report complete? Did you guys find something after all?"

"Uh, no." Martin's eyes evaded his friends'.

"Why the interest in that case?" Gregor asked.

"Oh, actually it doesn't interest me that much at all," Martin retorted. His answer sounded like a bad lie, because that's exactly what it was.

Luckily Gregor glanced at his watch just then. "Unfortunately I've got to get going. Do you want to grab a beer again sometime? Tomorrow, or the day after?"

Martin nodded, stepped out of his way, and exhaled as his friend jogged down the front steps.

"Can you manage OK by yourself from here?" Martin asked me, and I said yes. The sense of relief spreading through him overwhelmed me like a big, warm wave. That relief included his certain expectation that the natural place for me to sojourn would be here in the basement of this institute and that he would be freed from my presence once he left.

I let him persist in this belief for the time being.

My night was totally boring once again, the way nights do tend to be when you're surrounded by nothing but soulless corpses lying around. What, you didn't know? Eh, you haven't missed much. I tried to lure other wandering ghosts up and out, but I couldn't find any clues that other spirits were present. The question why I in particular was stranded here occupied me only briefly. I've never had much left over for philosophical crap, and so I preferred moldering around a little instead of seeking answers to the important questions of life and death.

Why the hell weren't there any TV sets down here, actually? Fine, the answer was admittedly obvious, because corpses stored in refrigerated morgue drawers typically do not require any diversion of that type. But now I found myself in a special situation, and I actually wouldn't have objected at all to having the constant, mind-numbing stream of the boob tube on for company, because sleep was out of the question. *Sleepless in Morgue Drawer Four*, I thought, trying to imagine how a romantic comedy could arise from this material, but I couldn't come up with anything. I think sawed-up corpses may not really make good stars for romantic comedies. As you can see, my thoughts were getting more and more idiotic, and just hanging out was getting more and more boring, so I went in search of a television. I found one in a conference room, but it was turned all the way off. So off that even the standby light wasn't on. Since I no longer possessed any fingers I might have used to depress the power button, I spent a while cooing around the beautifully designed appliance, but I soon had to concede this wasn't going to get my any further, and so I left the conference room. I had better luck in another room. There was a TV on standby. I tried to switch the set on with my electromagnetic waves—because I had heard about things like that at some point. Pulses of thought are really electromagnetic waves, or something along those lines. And things like cell phones, computers, and maybe, with just a little luck, televisions have something to do with those waves, too. So I focused my thoughts on switching the TV on. I don't want to bore you, so I'll briefly summarize the result of my efforts: it didn't work. Still, I'd killed some time (funny way to word that, don't you think?), and so now I didn't have to wait so long for the return of my noble forensic pathologist/knight.

———•———

At the start of the work day, Martin came into the basement and asked in his thoughts, Everything OK with you? And he then apologized that he had a ton of work to do and didn't have time for me just now. I felt his relief when I said that wasn't a problem, he shouldn't give any thought to me, just get his important work done. He trotted out, and I after him. Of course I should have left him in peace, but I already had a totally boring night behind me, and I wanted some action! I firmly resolved not to put him in any embarrassing situations, and I followed him without making myself noticed. And that ended up working out really well.

I've written hardly a positive word about Martin so far, and back at the moment when I started tailing him to escape my boredom I hadn't really anticipated feeling the need to do so, either. But now, since I've not only brought Martin's life to the brink of catastrophe but also put him right in the thick of things, I feel compelled to clear a few things up.

I'm sure you've had the experience of seeing someone you've never met before and just knowing at a glance if they're a cheerful or grumpy type. Martin is one of the cheerful ones. His face tells you right away that he likes to laugh, and the way his colleagues said hi to him on this morning showed me that people like him. A guy named Jochen came over to Martin's desk and laid an old, handled-to-death city map onto the desk, and he said he'd brought it back for Martin from his trip out of town over the weekend. Martin picked up the map, unfolded it, studied it, and thanked Jochen effusively.

"Where did you get it?" he asked.

"At the flea market," Jochen explained, his chest puffed out with pride.

(Yes, we're talking here about an old city map—a thing that shows streets and train lines and buildings and all that.)

"It's a true rarity," Martin said enthusiastically.

Jochen patted him on the shoulder again, assuring Martin that the pleasure was entirely his, and he accepted Martin's repeated thanks with a grin. If I still had a mouth, then it'd have been gaping so wide open you could shove an entire XXL Burger Value Meal sideways into it. With fries. And dessert. But I pulled myself together; I didn't want to irritate him, which was exactly why I had undertaken not to let him sense my presence, so I kept my trap shut. But it was hard, let me tell you.

The day had nothing interesting to offer; Martin wrote reports—or, more accurately: he dictated them. I had never seen something like that before, so I stayed with him for quite a while watching. His computer has a program that recognizes speech. Because I've learned what that means since then, obviously, I can quickly explain it to you now: you speak into the microphone attached to your headset, which is also connected to the computer, and then the computer types what you say all by itself. Crazy, right? Imagine a typing pool in an office, like at a lawyer's office or something. In the olden days the typists would all be putting their special finger skills to the test, but nowadays the women are all sitting there wearing headsets that ruin their hair, hands resting lazily in their laps, and they just mutter out their letters, memos, and reports, which the computers type. INSANE!

Anyways, Martin was prattling out his endless reports, and the computer was diligently taking everything down. Impressive technology. Of course, a proper soccer match would've held my attention more, and longer, but no one seemed to be using a computer for anything even remotely interesting in this office building. No softcore porn on the Internet, no hot chats with anonymous representatives of large religious communities, and no gambling. Not even harmless things like flight simulators or car racing. Just reports, reports, reports. So I soon lost interest and started cruising around the offices aimlessly, wiling away the time and finding my passive existence somewhat bleak. Sure, I was able to take a look around in the women's bathroom and stare at the women's panties without them noticing anything. I practiced going through the wall a bit and was happy about the slight tickle I felt when I whooshed through the wall into the break room and landed in the microwave. But I couldn't get a cup of coffee for myself—which, due to the tight spatial situation in front of the coffee machine, could've been pretty interesting at times. Specifically, if some piece of skirt were standing in this corner of the break room, there would basically be no way to avoid a full body check. The break room's interior designer must have been a pretty clever guy. Anyways, I'd have enjoyed squeezing past some lab coat booty in front of the coffee machine, but then I remembered: no body, no check. No luck!

Slowly the offices emptied out, and I peeked in on Martin again; at some point he also powered down his computer, grabbed his duffle coat, and made his way to the basement. With me quickly in tow. After we got downstairs I pretended I'd spent the whole day like a good boy in my morgue drawer and I was now extremely happy that someone had finally come to visit me. Martin fell for it.

"Martin," I said in a tone I hoped sounded trustworthy and serious, the way the news anchors on public television like to come off. "Now, finally, we really have to get cracking with our investigation, otherwise all our leads will be cold, and the truth about my murder will never come out."

I was proud of the seriousness of my statements and my absolutely professional diction. Of course, I was also just as proud of my self-control, because I'd actually spent a long time coming up with that until phrases such as "lazy pigs," "boil-ridden, rat-assed murderers," and the like stopped occurring to me.

Martin hemmed and hawed, writhing like an earthworm in between the blades of someone's garden shears.

"I'm not entirely certain whether . . ." His nicely preformulated sentence construction ended there, but since I could read the pulses from his brain clearly, I detected the rest of what he had wanted to say among the unraveling streams of thought: he didn't believe a single word in my entire story.

"Martin, where's the problem?" I asked, still under self-control and proud of it. I even used his name—did you notice?—because whenever you address someone by name, then you establish a certain connection with him. I learned that from a movie once.

"All investigations point toward your death being an accident. No one saw anyone push you."

"Martin," I said again. "Whether or not someone sees something doesn't matter. Look, if I weren't such a thorough person I wouldn't have seen the body in the trunk, either."

"What body?" Martin asked. "In what trunk?"

Now I totally wasn't expecting that. In my mind's eye— the only eye I still have—I quickly ran back through our previous conversations and realized I hadn't told Martin anything at all about stealing the car or the body in the trunk! I remedied that now as fast as I could.

Martin seemed totally distraught.

"OK, you see," I said, trying to get him back on track, "I discovered this body in the trunk only by accident."

Martin just couldn't grasp what I was trying to tell him. Oh my God, sometimes academics are really slow on the uptake.

I explained it again, enunciating clearly. "The body was in the trunk. I happened to look in there and find her. But the body would still have been in there if I hadn't checked. Then no one would have seen her, but she would still have been there."

Now I thought I had expressed myself quite clearly, but Martin was still hemming and hawing: "But if there was in fact a body, it would have had to turn up at some point here at the Institute."

I don't know what was wrong with Martin, but apparently he enjoyed having brain farts the minute anything even remotely had to do with me. I tried to explain it to him in simpler words.

"If your mother died, would you pack her into your trunk?" I asked.

"Of course not. She wouldn't even fit in there," he replied.

"But you wouldn't try to, either, right?" I asked with the patience of a saint (finally I know where that expression comes from—if only I still had adrenalin in my arteries . . .).

"No."

"What would you do?"

"Call the mortuary."

"AH HA!" We were slowly getting somewhere.

"So what do you think?" I continued, choosing my words carefully. "What might the reason be for someone to stash a body in the trunk of a car?"

"Her death hasn't been reported," he said after thinking a bit.

"Exactly!" I was relieved. He had managed to get there on his own. "And for what purpose does one stick an unreported dead body into the trunk of an automobile?"

"To take her somewhere and bury her in a shallow grave," Martin whispered.

Unfathomable. The man deals with unnatural deaths day in and day out, sees bodies that would make any other normal person's stomach and whatever else turn, but when it comes to imagining why such bodies end up on his autopsy table in the first place, he goes all wobbly-kneed.

"Exactly," I said, praising him. "The body may never turn up; that is exactly why the whole trunk procedure is used."

"Hmm."

"Also interesting is the question of where the car ended up."

"The car?"

We could have easily turned this conversation into a sit-com. Guaranteed to be a hit.

"That kind of car costs a half million euros. If it gets stolen, you report it to the insurance company, right?"

"I would certainly assume so."

Ah ha, we were again achieving complete sentences. Good.

"So, find out whether anyone has reported that kind of car stolen," I suggested.

"And if not?" Martin asked.

"Then it's because it had a body in the trunk, and people prefer to avoid mentioning that kind of thing on the incident report forms for the insurance."

He was not a hundred percent convinced, but I was sure he would look into it. And then he would finally start helping me solve my murder with a bit more conviction and verve. At least, I hoped so.

I considered riding home with him, but I decided to stay and try my luck with the TVs again. I'd hung out during the day for a while in the conference room while they were playing a video presentation, and I thought I could sense some of those waves. Maybe I could figure out how to get the TV to turn on. I accompanied Martin to the door and then made my way upstairs.

THREE

I'd hardly started making my way toward the TV when I heard a distant shriek for help. OK, fine—at first I wasn't sure if it really was a shriek for help or if some wave rushing through the area had upset my thoughts. After all, if you believe the people wearing aluminum-foil helmets, there are millions of radio, television, and of course cell phone signals flitting through the air all the time, so the likelihood that I might fly through one of those waves at some point and be able to interpret it was more than probable. At least, I thought so. Science wasn't really my kind of thing in school, but I had always liked the experiments with loud bangs, big whooshes, or bad smells. Although ultimately the question of *why* the bangs, whooshes, or smells occur always really irritated me.

Anyways, I focused my attention on what I thought I had heard, and in fact I heard the shriek again. Clearly a shriek for help. From Martin. Uh-oh, foul mischance!

I raced to the door that he had disappeared through and flashed through it as well without even looking for the crack or keyhole first. An ice-cold hurricane-force wind was whistling through the front courtyard—at least that's how it seemed to me. I was afraid. Afraid that the wind would just sweep me away somewhere I'd be all alone. Afraid I might even be blown apart and no longer exist—just like that, poof, Pascha's gone. Afraid of losing the rest of my wretched existence. I clung to my life, although it wasn't a real one anymore.

Martin was apparently also afraid, because although I couldn't hear him anymore I was receiving signals from him, and they were sheer terror. I whizzed in the direction I was getting the signals from, to the shoulder of the road where only a single wannabe car was parked: Martin's ugly little trash can. The lighting here wasn't the best; behind me was the Institute for Forensic Medicine and right next to that was Melaten Cemetery, a gruesome setting that might have sent a shiver down my spine if I had still had a back. Instead I focused on keeping all the molecules or whatever I was made of together and not letting myself be blown apart or away so I could make it to Martin, who was being pressed onto his car by a not very tall but extremely obese man.

"I'll cut your ugly pig ears off if you show up at my woman's place again asking stupid questions about that little chicken shit, got it?" the guy was just telling Martin.

Of course, it wasn't a real yes/no question—no one in that situation would answer no, and Martin didn't, either. He just nodded.

"Good. Then let's have a nice little chat, man to man, about what kind of shit you were trying to pull off at her place."

The guy was still leaning on the trash can car, and Martin was wedged in between it and him. He didn't look like he wanted to have a nice, man-to-man chat; he looked more like he really wanted to smash in the face of someone he considered cowardly and weaker than him, but I kept that observation to myself.

"I'm here," I said. "Stay cool, he's not going to do anything to you."

"Ha ha," Martin countered. "So he's just playing around?"

I was impressed. Having a sense of humor in a situation like this was evidence of a certain toughness that Martin otherwise seemed to totally lack. But maybe he was just slowly cracking up.

"If he'd wanted to kill you, you'd already be dead," I said to console him, but Martin's brain waves weren't calming down. To the contrary. Maybe I shouldn't have said the D-word out loud.

"What were you doing at my little lady's place?" the guy asked. His voice was so hoarse I was certain he'd expire from lung cancer long before his statistical life expectancy, but we didn't have time to wait for that.

"Bend his ears in your finest medical-doctorese and make clear to him that you were at Nina's as part of an official visit," I suggested. "Once he realizes you're a cop, he'll piss himself."

"I performed the postmortem on the body of Sascha Lerchenberg and in doing so was not able to resolve a few questions sufficiently," Martin began with all the authority he could muster. It was already quite a show; I was amazed. The response by the fat jellyfish was direct and unambiguous. He stood up straight, thereby releasing Martin's constrained body, and even took a step backward. Martin straightened his shoulders, which did not really look all that impressive in a duffle coat, and raised his chin.

"Body butchers don't do investigations," the jellyfish said in a tone I knew well. He was going to the trouble to sound self-confident and superior, but there was doubt there. I could hear it in him. Still, I was amazed that Nina had apparently noted both Martin's name and his mention of the Institute for Forensic Medicine, and the jellyfish seemed stupefied that the name and profession weren't a bluff. He tried not to let on about his surprise and accordingly kept jabbing his finger into Martin's chest when he spoke. But Martin pushed his hand away.

"Systemically inherent situational constraints have resulted with progressively increasing frequency in much more active involvement by forensic pathologists in the investigative work of our colleagues in criminal investigation units."

I thought maybe I hadn't heard him correctly. Martin had unleashed the full, unmitigated linguistic power of his medical education. Cool.

"But . . ." the jellyfish tried to blabber in between, but my forensic pathology adviser kept going right on at him, interlocuting as trenchantly as he cut.

"Multidisciplinary competencies have long formed part of the professional profile in academic environments, and this trend has been steadily gaining in relevance. Investigative teams today no longer consist solely of narrow-minded specialists. But if you have a problem with the management of the case-oriented knowledge here, you can file a complaint with the oversight board."

Wow! And he came up with that without even having to look anything up in a Latin dictionary. Point to Martin, but apparently he didn't quite know how to bring the matter to a victorious conclusion, because the jellyfish was still standing in front of him exuding aggression.

At first I kept my trap shut because I didn't really under-stand this situation. In my world an argument runs like this: two people one-up each other, the register of discourse declines a step with each additional utterance, and when there aren't any variations left of "rat-fucked elephant-cock-sucker," you duke it out. The version we had going here wasn't bad, either. I just couldn't predict what would come next. Jellyfish apparently didn't either: his crest began to deflate, if you'd like to phrase it poetically. And with that, Martin became master of the situation. Just by droning on! I think this was the very moment when my slow learning process with language truly began. After all, verbal com-munication was the only thing I still had going for me in my current form of existence. I couldn't ram my knee into someone's crotch, pick up a chick, or take part in any of the beautiful, purely physical forms of expression at all any-more. Language was the only thing I had left, and that's why I urgently needed to elevate this form of expression in myself above the three-hundred-word threshold that I had sunken into in recent years. Well, at the time I still lacked any epically broad awareness of all this, so please keep reading.

I'll omit the abundantly brainless "ums" and "hmms" that Jellyfish uttered—ultimately I don't want to bore you, and they didn't contribute much to the progress of the negotiation anyway.

"Your turn," I said at some point to Martin, who did not appear to have gotten that he was in charge.

"Let's get out of here," Martin thought, trying to go around the car to the driver's side. However, that was too abrupt for Jellyfish; he hadn't yet processed what Martin had said. He took another step forward.

"If you're looking for someone who had a burning hatred for Pascha, sir, then you should probably talk to Pablo," Jellyfish said. He'd managed to find his way to a new, more civilized mode of discourse after all, even addressing Martin as "sir."

"Your intended did mention that name," Martin said, and I swear on every beer I've ever downed that he actually said *intended*. "Is he that dealer?"

Actually all Martin wanted was to get away, but he's just so polite and doesn't interrupt a conversation midway through. Even if he's chatting with a small-time criminal who has just threatened to cut off his little pig ears.

"Exactly."

"I think he's in prison," Martin said.

"Not anymore," Jellyfish said, apparently feeling super stoked because he finally knew something that might be of interest. "Good behavior and all that shit. He's out. For the last two or three weeks or so."

"Thank you," Martin said, now pushing his way past the tub of lard to get into his car. I was quick to dart in, too, and looked back as Martin pulled out into traffic. My ex had clearly gone downhill, I thought. Her fat jellyfish just got blabbered down by a chubby little man in a duffle coat. Lame, Girl. Totally lame.

———•———

"You really kept on him," I said, and Martin turned the steering wheel the wrong way, almost taking out a guy on his bike. In my view that wouldn't have been a bad thing; bike riders in traffic are about as pleasant as boils in your armpit, but Martin would likely have viewed this differently.

"Oh God, you're here?" he moaned. And when I say he moaned, then that's what he did, because he didn't say anything out loud but only thought it, and in your thoughts you can also moan a short phrase like that. I figured he didn't have much of his eloquence left over. Maybe he had only a certain quantity available per day, and he had burned himself out between writing clever reports all day and now talking down the fat "I'll save the honor of my disreputable girlfriend" dude.

"I don't want to have anything to do with types like that," Martin said. "Investigations are for the police."

His voice was trembling a little, and the persuasiveness he had just been using to weave jargon and borrowed words into a delicate chain of language was flushed down the toilet. I vacillated between feeling irritated and sorry for him, though actually I was tending quite uncharacteristically toward feeling sorry, but in my situation that was not something I could really afford. If I were to pat his head and say everything will be OK and he didn't have to talk to that nasty scumbag anymore, then my case would never be resolved; a murderer would continue to walk free and—even worse—Cologne's alternative crowd would forever remember me as that floor gymnast who fell off the bridge totally drunk. So, stay firm, no feeling sorry.

"Weeping is for women, that's why they both start with *w*," I said—not very eloquent, I admit, but I'm also just starting to further my study of language. "So act like a man, and embrace challenge."

Big words that I got out of some made-for-TV movie. Presumably a movie where all the heroes were wearing cowboy hats and never walked on foot but only rode horseback.

But maybe also a movie where a totally regular citizen is under threat from some maniac, so for the first time in his life he rustles up his shotgun out of the sock drawer where it's been since his grandfather handed it down to him, and he suddenly turns into an ice-cold killer. Totally Hollywood in any case, and thus an excellent guide for how to behave in my current situation, traveling within a millimeter per hour of the velocity prescribed by the posted speed limit, sitting inside a rolling trash can weaving through a snow-covered Cologne with a duffle-coated forensic pathologist at the wheel. High time that I find my way back to reality.

"The police have decided to leave my murder not only unpunished but also uninvestigated," I said in a voice so chilling a Hollywood hero could not have been more ominous. "A human being with alcohol in his blood and the broken remains of a schnapps bottle in the pocket of his jacket apparently doesn't deserve any further consideration."

Of course I knew saying that stupid passive-aggressive stuff wasn't fair, first to the system in general, and second—and especially—to Martin personally, but I was desperate and determined to tighten any screw I could reach. And the only thing in reach was Martin, who was now zigzagging through traffic like a monkey on a scooter under fire all because his cell phone had started ringing.

"Gänsewein." He actually answered very nicely and courteously with his name—and he was following the moving-vehicle code to a T by using his hands-free device, to boot.

"Hi, it's Gregor. We had talked about grabbing a beer. How about now?"

"Um, well, you know, I'm not feeling very well right now . . ."

"Is everything OK, Martin? Are you sick?"

"No, I'm not sick," Martin said. His voice sounded like he had at least one bullet lodged in his diaphragm.

"Last night you were a bit off, too," Gregor said, sounding him out. "You can tell me if something's wrong. Is something not OK?"

"It's green," I interrupted, because the stoplight that had allowed him to stop and talk had since turned again.

"I know that it's green," Martin said out loud and irritated into the phone.

"What's that?" Gregor asked back.

"Nothing, just the stoplight is green," Martin replied. "So, everything is just fine with me, I'm just feeling a little wiped."

Yikes, he got "wiped" from me—it actually didn't belong in his vocabulary at all. Gregor pretended he hadn't noticed anything. "Well then, maybe tomorrow . . ."

"Hold on!" I yelled, and Martin gasped in fright.

"What it is?" Gregor called, apparently highly alarmed by the frightened gasp. Presumably he suspected an accident or something.

"What about the SLR?" I asked.

"The SLR?" Martin echoed.

"What did you say?" Gregor asked.

"You wanted to ask him whether an SLR had been reported stolen," I reminded Martin.

"Say, do you know if a Mercedes SLR was reported stolen last week?" Martin babbled obediently into his headset. He had apparently lost all will to argue with me.

"No idea," Gregor answered. "Why are you interested in that?"

"Do me a favor and check, OK?" Martin asked in a voice underlain with deep exhaustion.

It was quiet on the line for a moment, and then Gregor asked Martin to wait for a second, and we could hear some mumbling in the background, and then he got back on the phone.

"No SLR has been reported stolen in Cologne. Not last week, not the week before, and not since. Tomorrow will you let me in on why you want to know that?"

"Yes, yes," Martin answered, then mumbled another thank-you and hung up.

"You see?" I asked triumphantly. "People who have bodies in their trunks don't report their cars ripped off."

"Maybe the reason why no theft was reported was precisely because there was no theft," Martin retorted.

"But . . ." I couldn't fathom the new direction our conversation had suddenly taken.

"You told me about a theft and a body. Maybe one of the two is incorrect, maybe both are incorrect. In any case I still have no evidence to support your story."

This whole discussion proved only one thing: that Martin was pretty clever.

We spent the rest of the ride in silence. Martin was driving like a robot, and as far as I could tell, he wasn't thinking anything. His brain was switched off. By contrast, I was mad. I was making an effort to pump all of the energy from my frustration into the convolutions of Martin's brain, but I couldn't tell if he noticed. He was on autopilot; maybe he was in shock.

———•—•———

He parked his "car" along a quiet side street, shut it off, and dragged his feet along the sidewalk. The door to another parked car opened, Martin took a frightened leap to the side but then relaxed a bit again as he recognized the person getting out.

"Birgit! What are you doing here?"

She beamed at him; I could only gape. Her naturally blond hair fell long and smooth and shiny over the fur collar of an orange-colored winter jacket, which, unfortunately, concealed her upper torso under a bulky mass of down. Her legs were inside black pinstriped pants that ran down to black high heels. Unless her jacket was covering up some monstrous deformity, the woman had to be pretty hot. Not quite as hot as her colleague, Katrin, but still. How had Martin landed this knockout?

"I wanted to show you my new car," she called in high spirits, hugging Martin briefly, and then hopping back across the sidewalk and opening her passenger side door for him. "Hop in."

Martin sighed softly but sat down on the leather seat like a good boy.

"What did you do with your old Polo?" he asked.

Totally unreal: this question was so unbelievably wrong at this point in time. When someone shows off their new car for you, then you ask how many horse the thing has under its hood, if the suspension is lowered, how many watts the system serves up, and if the maximum speed shown on the speedometer is correct. You don't ask what you did with your old car. And then just a Polo! Is there anything more trivial in life than the whereabouts of an old Polo?

"I sold it," Birgit mumbled. "I've always wanted to have one of these."

"Mmm hmm," was all Martin could contribute. I suspect he still didn't get what "one of these" actually meant. A BMW 3-Series convertible from the early 1980s, tiptop condition, grey exterior, red leather interior. Yeah, red! A totally awesome chick magnet. But Martin was sitting on the soft leather like a stuffed dummy, staring straight ahead, making an effort to smile and finally nodding.

"Nice," he said.

"Martin!" I screamed. "The thing is not 'nice,' it's kick-ass fresh."

"Kickass fresh," Martin repeated.

Birgit's grin widened. "You think?"

That's how you talk to chicks!

"Yes," Martin said. He was acting like he'd downed a whole box of psychiatric meds.

"I'm glad," Birgit cheered. "Should we go for a little spin?"

Martin shook his head. "Please don't be mad, but I'm not doing that well today. I've got a headache." Goodness gracious me, dear Martin was out of sorts!

"Another time, then," Birgit said, softening her tone.

There was a short pause.

"Do you want to come up?" Martin asked.

I was amazed. That was even better, of course. Instead of adrenalin in the car, right to testosterone in the love nest. I was experiencing excited anticipation, but I kept my mouth shut.

"Sure."

We got out of the car, climbed up to the third floor, and walked into Martin's apartment. Birgit apparently knew her way around, and Martin disappeared into the kitchen.

"Would you like some tea?" he called.

"Please."

What planet had I landed on? You drink tea when you're sick. I mean, really sick. Really suffering. Puking and the runs and all that. And the first thing that you try is actually Coke, everyone knows that. But when the cholera or whatever causes such messy business has been sticking around for a while, then you switch to tea. In the face of death, and definitely not together with a chick on your couch before you get down to business. But, please, I was familiarizing myself with an entirely new world, here. A parallel universe. I was actually excited to see how things would proceed.

Martin steeped loose-leaf tea, which he had to fuss with to measure out and fill into an environmentally friendly reusable tea filter and then dispose of in the compostable-waste container. I wondered what humanity had actually invented the teabag for.

I left Martin back in the kitchen and made my way to Birgit in the living room. When I entered the room, I had a massive shock. Fine, I wasn't really expecting Martin to hang his walls full of titty calendars, but what I found here totally shocked me. There were city maps hanging everywhere. Yeah, we encountered that already, do you remember? His colleague Jochen and the city map? So here's where that thread finds its resolution: Martin collects city maps. Old ones and up-to-date ones. The old ones were hung behind glass on his walls. I know I personally have always wanted to see what the streets of Cologne's medieval downtown used to be called, like, three hundred years ago. It's totally amazingly interesting, don't you think?

Birgit studied Cologne, Nürnberg, and Berlin—maybe she was learning a couple of street names by heart so that she could chat about them with Martin after he came back in. But maybe she was also wondering what was up with his oddball hobby, I couldn't tell. I swirled around her the way those famous moths do to light, but I couldn't establish any contact. Too bad. Really, really too bad.

Martin poured the tea in authentic style from a silver teapot into delicate little porcelain cups that were so thin you could almost see through them. The lady took milk. The Queen of England and her difficult family members would definitely have had fun with this game. Fortunately there was no extending of pinkies, otherwise I'd have virtually puked, and I was afraid that would not have improved Martin's state of mind. At the moment he wasn't noticing me, and that was certainly a good thing.

"How are things going at the bank?" Martin asked after he had doped himself up with a couple sips of tea.

Bank! I wouldn't have thought that of Birgit. Financial types are the absolute worst. Those arrogant pricks who jump into banking and finance programs right out of school all pretty much look like they take a swim every morning in a gigantic tub of lube. Even before starting their training at all! And after a couple of months in banking and finance their brains turn so mushy the only things they can still talk about are customers' current-account portfolios, tax on the interest on income from wheel bolt sales, or line-of-credit-compliant correlation. Worst of all, of course, they think they're the kings of the banking system, while in reality they're commercial-paper tigers. They're so dumb they put a DO NOT DISTURB sign on top of their phones during their lunch breaks and wonder why the phone still rings.

"Oh, pretty well," said Birgit, who was actually acting like a normal person and not like a malfunctioning computer. "We just wrapped up a giant piece of business with Saudi Arabia, which is why we've all been doing so much overtime lately."

Deliriously interesting what all the nation's intellectual elite spouts forth upon the chesterfield when getting together after work for a little cup of tea. No wonder the mood in Germany never really goes up. And surely with this kind of intellectual prattle as a mating dance our declining birthrate should be no surprise.

"So, anything exciting going on at work for you lately?" Birgit asked. And then presumably picturing what Martin does she started making a silly, nervous giggle.

I immediately found her much nicer—all the dead-serious conversation had been getting to me.

"I'm sorry; I'm still not used to your job."

Ah ha, they hadn't known each other that long. We were still in the warm-up phase of the relationship. I wanted to seize onto hope, but then I looked at Martin with his little porcelain teacup and his neatly parted hair sitting on the couch, the legs of his creased pants pulled up slightly so that the material around the knees wouldn't be baggy— nope, this wasn't going anywhere.

"Well, things are fairly routine at work," Martin said tamely. "However, I think I'll be standing in line for unemployment pretty soon if Dr. Eilig gets his bill through the Bundestag to ban autopsies."

"Oh, him, 'Dr. Christian,'" Birgit said, making a dismissive gesture with her hand. "That jack-in-the-pulpit is crazy," she said. "If it were up to him, doctors wouldn't be allowed to write any prescriptions for contraceptives anymore, and he wants to completely ban abortions as well, even when the life of the mother is at risk. He's not getting that bill through. Especially because he lacks so much credibility what with all the Mustangs and Lamborghinis and other outrageous cars he drives."

"I hope so," Martin said, "because otherwise with this reversion to the Dark Ages we'll be proof positive that Einstein was right after all about the relativity of time."

Good grief, here are two people in love sitting on the couch and, instead of fooling around some, they're driveling on about Einstein's theory of relativity. "Relative" described only one thing going on here: the degree of insanity in this situation, and it was pretty high.

Birgit dismissed his pessimism with her hand.

"Do you guys actually get updates from the police on the progress of investigations in murder cases?" she asked.

Martin nodded. "Typically we work very closely with the detectives, and they let us know when there are suspects. Sometimes we have to do special investigations or provide assessments to find out whether a certain suspect might in fact be a perpetrator. That means running DNA analyses or things like that."

Martin was a little distracted, but maybe Birgit wasn't noticing that at all. I hadn't checked yet how well the two of them really knew each other, and in the case of Birgit I obviously didn't know what was going on inside her head, either. Maybe more physics of love than physics of time?

"Do you think your work is actually fun, or do you do it because someone has to do it?" she asked.

"Normally it's fun for me," Martin mumbled.

"Normally?"

Martin poured a warm-up into their teacups, drawing the ceremony out ridiculously long.

"I've just had a case where I don't know exactly what I should do," he finally said.

I pricked up my ears, so to speak.

"Do tell," Birgit encouraged him enthusiastically, scooting a bit closer. Even without knowing her innermost thoughts, any blind person could see that she was totally into Martin. He presumably needed only flick his finger and she would pounce on him. But he didn't flick, he sipped. Tea. Then things continued.

"There is a body that I examined briefly at the site where it was found and later autopsied," Martin explained in his doctor's voice. "There isn't any real evidence of foul play, actually."

"Actually . . ." Birgit said, helping him along. She was literally quivering with curiosity about an exciting story.

Personally I'd have done something different with a quivering babe on the couch than tell her about dead bodies—but to each his own.

"In retrospect I've got a strange feeling that something is not right about this death," Martin mumbled.

He'd come up with a really nice way to word it so that he didn't have to say that the restless soul of a dead man has been jabbering his ears off.

"What kind of feeling?" Birgit asked.

She was so fascinated by the story that her cheeks were all flushed and her lips slightly open. She was staring at Martin with wide eyes. If only I still had even a couple little hormones left . . . But I was surprised, and specifically at Martin. He just kept on chattering at her about this grizzly corpse he'd examined.

"Well, it's just a feeling," he said.

Of course that way of phrasing it was completely unhelpful, but apparently he didn't under any circumstance intend to say what was really going on with him. "That's exactly the problem," he quickly continued. "I can't prove anything. There's no evidence from the body that it didn't fall accidentally but was pushed. Apparently there weren't any clues along those lines at the site, so the police aren't continuing the investigation. The case is closed."

"You just have the impression that something else is going on," Birgit said, ending his summary.

Martin nodded.

"And it's bugging you."

Again an observation, not a question.

More nodding, more sipping.

"Well, then look into it," Birgit recommended, short and sweet.

I could have kissed her. Well, I wanted to anyways, but even more so after this recommendation.

Martin bowed his head.

"Officially I'm not allowed to do anything at all," Martin said.

"But you are allowed to ask around a little, as long as you're not acting like you're doing an official investigation in your capacity as a coroner for the city attorney," she retorted.

Not dumb at all. No, she wasn't putting a little sign on her phone at lunch, I was sure of that.

"But why should I do that when there isn't any evidence at all?" Martin asked, almost resigned.

"Because you'll never find peace," Birgit said, obviously without even the slightest idea how entirely true her assessment was.

Martin just moaned loudly, but quickly pulled himself together and said, "No, you're right. It'll keep gnawing at me." He said "it," but he meant "he." And he was damned right. I'd keep setting fire under his ass until I found out who killed me, and I thought I had a certain justification in doing so. Of course, it was too bad for Martin that I could make contact specifically, and unfortunately only, with him, but it was too bad for me, too. I'd have picked a somewhat gutsier helper. Or a female one. Birgit. Or Katrin. But I had gotten stuck with a trash can driver. A duffle coat wearer. Tea drinker. Bean counter. City map collector. Presumably also a muesli eater, gravesite tender, and sock darner. What had I done to deserve this?

"It's really bugging you, isn't it?" Birgit asked, putting her hand on Martin's cheek. I could feel Martin's heart surge. For me it'd have been more like a knife in my pants, but Martin, my Little Goose, was made of different material.

"Should we go grab a bite to eat?" she suggested.

Martin shook his head. "I'm sorry, Birgit, but I'm afraid I'm really not up for anything today."

Birgit was a good loser. "All right. I'll head home then. But my invitation to dinner is just postponed, not rescinded."

Invitation! The amazing things that emancipated womenfolk come up with. Maybe I should've found myself some kind of modern chick like this. And if they even pay for their own food . . .

72

She left; Martin made himself a light dinner of a slice of bread with some snot-green vegetarian paste smeared on it, and he actually brought himself to eat that crap. But for someone who earns his money carving up bodies, there probably isn't really any such thing as revolting. I took a look around the apartment, noting that the furniture everywhere was modern with a bit of an Asian bent and that there was no TV in the bedroom. Instead: a stationary bike. Ugh, how healthy!

Martin had turned the TV in the living room on and was watching the news.

"Change the channel," I urged him.

Martin dropped the remote in terror. I had been completely off his radar.

"You're still here!"

"Would you prefer I had left with Birgit? Now change the channel!"

"What to?"

"Doesn't matter, just not the news. It always puts me to sleep."

"That'd be OK by me," Martin said.

He kept watching the news, but he was distracted.

"We should find Pablo and talk to him," I suggested. If there wasn't any reasonable television programming to watch, we might as well do some more investigating.

"There is no way I am going out right now in the dark looking for a dealer generally presumed to be a murderer," Martin responded.

Somehow war scenes were showing on the screen, and I wondered again why reporters risk their lives every day to take stupid images like these. Year after year, people snuffing each other out always looks the same. Admittedly, sometimes the parties involved have slanted eyes or black skin, sometimes the uniforms are beige, brown, or green, but in principal the scenes are all the same. I had long ago given up watching that crap.

"Birgit thinks you shouldn't just let the case slide, either," I reminded him.

"Leave Birgit out of it."

"You were the one who told her the story, not me," I made clear.

"I have left work for the day," Martin grumbled. He had since scarfed down his snot-paste sandwich.

"It's a good thing you're off work now because during working hours you can't investigate anything very well," I retorted.

"No hunting for dealers," Martin persisted.

I thought for a moment.

"It occurred to me that Mehmet may be my murderer," I said.

"Who is Mehmet?" Martin asked.

"The guy from the game hall I owed money to."

"Mmm hmm."

"A game hall is an extremely safe place," I clarified.

"Mmm hmm."

"And Mehmet is a really nice guy."

Martin closed his eyes, rested his face in his hands, paused for a moment, and then switched the TV off. "All right. So where is this game hall?"

I guided him through traffic, steering him into the side streets where I'd always used to park, and I recommended he leave the car here. He had safety-related concerns.

"Nothing has ever happened to my ride around here," I said.

"What kind of a car did you use to have?" he asked.

"A VW Scirocco R."

Martin didn't say anything, he just snorted slightly through his nose and did not seem very reassured. In the field of automobile valuations he was apparently seriously deficient. All the same, he parked under a streetlight without any further discussion, carefully locked up, and pulled up his duffle coat hood for the short walk. It was drizzling. I found it very disconcerting to see the rain but not feel it.

"Good evening," Martin said to everyone and no one in particular, as well-mannered Germans do, when he entered the establishment.

About six pairs of eyes gawked at him in disbelief.

"Whatcha wanna play?" Mehmet asked, standing at the coffee machine as Martin walked up to him.

"I've got a question," Martin said.

"The million-euro question?" Mehmet smirked. "Do you have an 'ask the audience' lifeline left?"

The boys at the pool table laughed; the gambling addicts on the slot machines were, as usual, so deeply lost in their games that they hadn't caught any of this.

"Did you know Sascha Lerchenberg?" Martin asked after smiling at Mehmet's joke.

"Who wants to know?"

"A friend," Martin answered, and I thought that answer was right on; Mehmet gaped at the man in the little wool coat in disbelief. Then his face darkened.

"What do you mean '*did* you know'?" he asked.

"He's dead."

I had assumed Mehmet would now offer his condolences about my death and say what a nice guy I'd been, which is why at first I thought I'd misheard when Mehmet loudly spit out, "That bastard!"

I was speechless.

"Why do you say that?" Martin asked, and again I had to admire him. In situations where any normal person would just come in arms swinging, Martin was as cool as a deep-frozen fish stick.

"Because he owes me money," Mehmet said.

"I'm certain he didn't intentionally cause his own death just to leave you with a financial shortfall," Martin said, choosing his words carefully, and I confirmed this with a loud yes.

"Intentional or not, man, what kind of shit are you trying to pull here?" Mehmet asked in a tone that I did not like at all. "Money is money, and gone is gone."

"Had the news of his death not yet been brought to your attention?" Martin asked, and Mehmet hesitated for a moment before it clicked what we wanted to know from him.

"I hadn't heard anything," Mehmet replied.

"We believe him," I told Martin.

"Why?" Martin asked me back, in his head.

"Because Mehmet stinks like an Middle Eastern whorehouse without running water, and I would definitely remember getting a whiff of him if he had been the one behind me on the bridge."

Martin nodded.

"Who'll be paying me the money now?" Mehmet asked.

The boys at the pool table had since interrupted their game and were eavesdropping on the conversation. I tried to draw this to Martin's attention, but his head was full of other thoughts.

"I don't know," Martin said seriously. "Possibly his next of kin . . ."

"Do you think I'm going to write a sympathy card to his mama and explain how her son has illegal-gambling debts at my joint, and please could she have her bank wire the dough to my public assistance account?" Mehmet roared.

"No, of course not," Martin said meekly.

Martin hadn't considered this problem. In our circles you don't issue criminal debentures at a fixed interest rate and with a processing fee, and most debts—since they were never officially made—you can collect on only from the actual debtor.

"Well, then . . ." he said.

"Let's get going," I suggested, looking around at the shooters, who weren't playing anymore. Apparently Martin didn't hear me.

"There is evidence that someone aided in Pascha's death," Martin said. "Would you have an idea who might have wished him dead?"

"Apart from me, you mean, Kewpie Face?" Mehmet asked.

"Martin!" I screamed. "Retreat!"

"Well, certainly, it might have been an accident after all," Martin backpedaled. Apparently he was slowly getting that the topic of discussion here had been exhausted. "Thank you very much for your patience."

Martin stepped to the side to avoid running into the two pool players and left the game hall.

"We can cross that off the list, too," he said. "If this Mehmet has always struggled with cologne abuse, then we might have spared ourselves the trip."

"Yeah, that's true. But I just didn't remember that at all," I said, and that was the pure truth.

We went back to Martin's car. Unfortunately a nasty surprise was waiting for us there in the form of the two pool players from Mehmet's house of fortune, who were leaning casually on the trash can. I had actually forgotten that the game hall had a back exit. Shit! In Martin's thoughts I saw the question arise how these guys knew that this was his car, and I kept the tip-off to myself that a guy with nicely parted hair but no hair gel, and in a duffle coat but no discernible gold jewelry, would be the one and only male suspect within a range of about two thousand meters of being the driver of this roofed-over geriatric walker. At the moment we had other problems, anyways.

The two muscle mountains didn't say anything at first, calmly puffing on their smokes and acting like they hadn't noticed Martin at all. Martin hesitated about four meters away from his car. Then he shrugged and went at it.

"Excuse me, but would you mind letting me get into my car?" he asked the first muscle mountain—for simplicity's sake let's just call him King, to be nice. King didn't do anything.

"First we would need to clear something up," the second guy mumbled, who we'll call Kong.

"I think everything has been cleared up," Martin said. "Pascha suffered a regretful accident and died from his injuries."

He got that out in a really convincing way, although I hoped he had since stopped believing it was an accident and embraced with considerable certainty that I am not wholly and entirely dead.

"Debts don't die as fast as people," Kong mumbled softly in no direction in particular.

"Unfortunately, I am unable to assist you further in this delicate matter," Martin said in a firm voice. I still had not decided if he really was slow on the uptake or was just hoping consistent denial would get him out of the situation unperturbed.

"You come over here asking dumb questions," Kong muttered on. "Because you," he paused, "are a friend of Pascha's." Martin sensibly kept his trap shut. "But you seem like," again a pause, "a man of honor."

King choked on the smoke from his foul-smelling cigarette. "Man of honor, yeah right," he gasped.

I hoped his face would get a little redder and he'd keel over dead, but he didn't do me the pleasure. Too bad, since the dramatic demise of an adversary was always the climax of the action flicks I used to love. And it usually helps get the hero out of his current predicament, too. We could have used help like that just now, and it wouldn't have been that sad to see this dope done for, but, as I said, he didn't do us the pleasure. He coughed again and then regained his composure.

"I would really like to get into my car and drive home," Martin said quietly.

"We're coming along," Kong said.

King nodded.

"Certainly not," Martin said.

"Not to your house," Kong confirmed. "Just to the closest ATM."

I think that by now Martin could clearly see which way the wind was blowing.

"What amount are we talking about?" he asked.

"Three thousand," said Kong.

"Bullshit," I yelled in between. "I owed Mehmet one thousand nine hundred and not one eurocent more."

"First of all, that's a lie, and second of all, you're welcome to get in the car with me, but then we'll be driving to police headquarters where my colleagues there will be able to take down your complaint about a theft," Martin said.

"We're not filing any complaints, asshole," King roared.

"You can tell the lady who cleans your toilet all about your colleagues," Kong muttered. "Give him the key." He pointed to King.

"No," Martin said.

I could feel his fear, but as a scientist he was able to evaluate the consequences of potential actions on his own, and it was clear to him we wouldn't be able to get rid of these two characters at all if he handed over the key now.

"No problem," King said, smashing in the driver's side window.

"Hey, stop that!" Martin yelled.

A car thief with any pride at all is not in the habit of stealing French-made toy trash can cars, which is why King didn't know any of the tricks for opening the door in a flash, and he didn't have a tool with him. So we had a tiny bit of time to convince the two bruisers that they had better not lay into the chubby little man in the bulky little coat. As fast as I could, I ran down all the information I had about Mehmet and his illegal gambling operation and implored Martin, if his life meant anything to him, to just talk them to death now. And he obeyed instantly.

"Mehmet ought to be keeping things a bit more discreet," Martin's mouth quacked obediently. "The regular visitors to his back room would surely not appreciate it if, at five tomorrow morning, the police disturbed their beauty sleep and started asking questions about certain 'gentlemen's events.'"

Kong was the smarter of the two. He visibly winced. That this little man standing in front of him knew anything at all about the back room was a shock. But now we were just getting started.

"The poker round last Thursday was illegal solely on the basis that it was 'gambling for money,'" Martin adlibbed, based on what I was dictating. "Quite apart from the fact that a felon with an open arrest warrant was in attendance, who additionally attempted to engage in the illegal 'procuration of women for immoral purposes.'"

Kong took a step back; King still had his hand on the driver's side door. He didn't move.

"Who are you?" Kong asked.

Martin was able to suppress his instinct to answer the question properly the way his mommy taught him just in the nick of time. Instead, he continued to recite the script I was feeding him.

"Then there is the delicate matter of Mehmet operating the back room without the knowledge of the game hall's owner, which is putting him into a pretty shitty situation." The word "shitty" was hard for Martin to get past his lips, but he made an effort.

"Are you a cop?" Kong said in a renewed attempt to put his relationship with Chubby onto a more familiar basis by getting to know him better.

"Shut up," I said, and Martin actually repeated me! And this time without hesitation and with amazing intensity. And then all on his own he said it again: "Shut up." Then he turned to King. "Take your hand off of my car, take three steps backward, and let me go before I unload my knowledge about Mehmet at another location."

I was impressed. He definitely had a long fuse, but when you finally got his ass in gear even Martin the Gosling could turn into a rapacious bird of prey. Well, almost.

King gawked at Kong, who nodded, and the two withdrew. Martin unlocked the trash can and laid in a pretty smooth racing start.

"Hey, nicely done," I exclaimed. "You really showed them."

"Shut up," Martin shouted at me.

He was still in the rush of his newly found register.

"It's me, Pascha," I reminded him in the hope we would now resume talking to each other like two reasonable people.

"Exactly, Pascha. Shut up."

Somehow he was pissed off, and somehow at ME! But I hadn't smashed in his stupid window. Quite the contrary. I had supplied him with the ammunition that got him out of that sticky situation. And instead of thanking me, he was chewing me out. Again! I was insulted and didn't say anything else.

He drove to the Institute, opened the door, said good night, and vanished. I disappeared into my morgue drawer and sulked.

FOUR

I just dozed the whole night and only really came to again when the first couple of morgue drawers pulled open. There were two new arrivals, and one body was taken out of the morgue drawer at the upper left and served up for its postmortem. And then a fresh body arrived that was wheeled straight into the autopsy room. I wasn't particularly interested in all that today; I was still in a bad mood. For me, Mehmet was not out of the running as the murderer. Not after that encounter with his two pool-playing gorillas. Mehmet himself couldn't have pushed me from the bridge; as I said, I would have gotten a whiff of him even at two hundred meters against the wind what with the cloud of perfume around him that was as unrelenting as it was nauseating. But he might well have sicced his two rabid gorillas on me. It wasn't entirely clear to me what he hoped to gain by doing that, because a dead debtor can't pay back his debts, but who knew what exactly was really going on in the cerebral gyri of other people. Anyways, I hadn't checked him off my list just yet.

And the fat jellyfish who's been fooling around with my ex lately? What did I know about him? Nothing other than that he was horrifically flabby. And that was a far cry from saying that he couldn't have been a murderer, too. He'd just be a flabby murderer then—so what?

The fact was that I still didn't have the foggiest who had pushed me from the bridge onto the sidewalk and thereby promoted me from life to death, and this slight disgruntlement between Martin and me was definitely not helping solve the crime. So I had to make sure he started talking to me in full sentences again and not just in demands of dubious amicability, such as: "Shut up."

I spirited through the offices and break rooms looking for him, but I couldn't find him anywhere. I was afraid he was in the autopsy room dissecting bodies. I wasn't actually that interested in all the snip-snip stuff, but on the other hand I was really restless and wanted to make up with Martin again as soon as possible. So I jetted down there.

With the caps and face masks and gowns, all the figures around the stainless-steel tables looked pretty much alike, but Martin's chubby form was easy to pick out, and his brain waves ultimately navigated me to the right table. I made an effort not to notice the body lying there.

"Hello, Martin," I said.

"I'm very busy," Martin's thoughts told me, handling his scalpel with skillful precision. On the other side of the table there was a masked figure babbling all their findings into a dictation device. The jabbering distracted me a little, but I made an effort to concentrate on Martin.

"I'm sorry about last night," I said. One could construe that as an apology, perhaps even as a confession of guilt, although it wasn't supposed to be either. I was just hoping that Martin would soften up.

"I would hope so," he replied instead.

So much for hoping for a painless reconciliation. Apparently I needed some heavier artillery.

"You really did a great job pulling that off last night," I started. "I never expected two bruisers to be out there waiting to smash your window in."

Martin mumbled "hmm," but otherwise kept his attention strictly trained on the body.

"I'm really sorry, and I'd like to apologize that you came into contact with guys like that and that your car was damaged. All because of me."

Now I had confessed considerably more guilt than I had planned, but Martin was really being very aloof today. I was slowly getting mad. He should fucking accept my apology and stop being such a sorehead. Dumbass.

"I've got to concentrate here," Martin said.

A smooth rebuff. The kind I hated even when I was alive. My father was especially good at that. You come to someone with a totally important thing that can't be put off, and he just says "hmm" three times and that he doesn't have any time. Makes me puke. That's why I had to leave home at the time. And now Martin was starting with the same thing. My patience was again being put to the acid test.

"Martin!" I yelled to finally get him to pay attention to me. "Martin, I'm desperate!"

Now, I thought, he really had to react. A person like him can't just close his heart to that kind of cry for help, I thought.

Thought wrong. He didn't budge at all.

I spun around myself a couple of times to let off some of my anger and not shoot some kind of pulse wave into his skull and instantly destroy all the convolutions in his brain. But then exactly the one thing I had gone to great pains to avoid the whole time ended up happening: I caught a glimpse of the body that under Martin's hands was currently metamorphosing into a rotten-meat gyro. I shrieked.

I had completely suppressed the tattoos on the body's ankles, but as I saw them now I remembered.

"That's her!" I yelled. "Martin—that's the woman from the SLR!"

Now I had him. His attention was all mine. He folded the face of the woman back up again (please don't make me go into detail, but I'll say this much: during an autopsy the skin over the skull is cut from ear to ear and folded forward and backward . . .), he stared at her face for a moment, and asked: "Are you sure?"

"Yes," I said, but Martin presumably didn't get that at all because the person standing opposite him with the dictation device was staring at him surprised and asked what was wrong. Obviously that guy hadn't been privy to our conversation, and instead just saw Martin suddenly pause in mid-snip to smooth out the body's face and stare at it. It was certainly understandable that this would strike him as a bit odd, but that guy was really getting on my nerves because he was drawing Martin's attention away from the body and me again.

"I suddenly had the impression that I may have seen this woman before," Martin said.

"You didn't get that impression before we started, when you first looked at the face, but only now that you're making incisions around her kidneys?" his colleague asked quizzically.

"Uh, yes." Martin didn't say anything else—anything else would presumably have been used against him.

"And?" his colleague asked again. "Do you know her or not?"

"Uh, no."

"Can we continue, then?"

Martin nodded and returned to the offal that his likewise-masked dissector was delicately and cleanly separating and handing to him for diagnosis. Meanwhile I was somewhat starting to understand who does what during an autopsy, but of course at the moment that didn't interest me at all.

"Who is she?" I asked Martin.

"Jane Doe," he replied in his businesslike voice.

"What did she die of?" I asked.

"We don't know yet."

"But you'll find out?"

Martin nodded. "The district attorney ordered the whole gamut."

"What gamut?" I didn't have the foggiest idea what he was talking about.

"We're doing a full postmortem, including DNA and tox screen."

He must have sensed my next question before I could even ask it because he immediately explained, "There will be a genetic examination and a toxicological examination. The crime scene investigation unit has already removed any potential external evidence on the body, and that will be examined by their forensic technicians."

"Where was she found?" I asked.

"No idea. But she was lying outside for a few days," Martin said. "There are signs of bites . . ."

"She wasn't injured when I saw her," I interjected.

". . . signs of bites by animals, which happened because she was outside."

I thanked him profusely and withdrew into my drawer. He could go to hell with his "signs of bites," as far I was concerned. I truly didn't need to know everything. The fact that the body of the woman from the stolen car had turned up gave me plenty of material to think about. Now finally there was a piece of evidence that my story was true. Provided, of course, that Martin and his colleagues found evidence to confirm my story. Otherwise he would just say again that I could have invented everything and simply identified any old body as the dead woman from the trunk. I had no idea how much information can come out of an "autopsy, including DNA and tox screen," but I really hoped with all my heart that Martin would finally believe me and continue our investigation.

If not, I would probably be stuck here in the basement of the Institute for Forensic Medicine for all eternity, begging generations of coroners to review the case of Sascha a.k.a. Pascha Lerchenberg . . . What a horrific idea!

Of course, I could tell I was slowly working myself up into a certain hysteria, but being aware of a mental overreaction does not necessarily mean that you can just set it all aside. To the contrary. Realizing that your psychological balance is severely disturbed quickly results in feeling even worse, even more pessimistic, and even sorrier for yourself. And that's exactly what I was doing. Big time. I was wallowing in self-pity until at some point I was so bad off I would really have liked to sob. But how?

Instead a kind of shame suddenly overcame me. Really. I wouldn't have expected it, either, but in fact I was ashamed of being a wimp. Even so, I wasn't the only one who'd had a rough time the past few days. The woman getting the deli-slice treatment from Martin right now was also dead. And she had even more reason to complain. She wasn't just a dead woman, but an anonymous body. No one had any idea who she was. Did she have a family who should be informed? Was she married, with children—who would now be half-orphans? She was such a burden to the person she was last with that he buried her anonymously, intending to leave her friends and family in eternal uncertainty. And then she also kind of became a victim again when I stole the car, and then she was disposed of like garbage for a second time. Human garbage that had been unloaded somewhere and eaten away at by animals. A nauseating end. Worse then mine. Truly.

I decided to include her in my investigation. That is, in the investigation of my case that Martin was supposed to be doing. And with that decision I returned to where my line of thought had begun: Martin simply had to help me. Maybe I could stir him up more with the sappy story of the anonymous dead woman. I would at least try.

The autopsy room had since emptied out, and I was relieved. Presumably my intrepid forensic pathologist was now sitting at his desk, nibbling on a baby carrot (he actually did that on occasion to fend off hunger in between meals) and writing whatever boring reports again. I whooshed out to find him.

He wasn't at his desk, maybe . . . I hesitated. On his computer that program was running that he uses to dictate reports. I was already quite familiar with the icon showing his mic wasn't turned all the way off but was just asleep.

That means you just need to speak a command to reactivate it, and you can start chattering on again. I proceeded to the mouthpiece on the headset and intensely thought: activate microphone.

Nothing happened. I thought the command several times more, sometimes slower, sometimes faster, but always very clearly and distinctly. I don't know exactly how to express it, but I was phrasing it at Martin's pitch, so to speak. Still nothing happened. I was frustrated. All those famous electromagnetic waves or pulses, or God only knows what those nasty little things are called, they just did not seem to want to do what I wanted them to. That's how it used to be in chemistry class, or when we would do physics experiments—and let's just not even talk about gym at all. Presumably the deep-seated trauma from gym class was the only thing that really connected Martin and me, because the way he looked and moved I was sure he was always the last guy chosen for a team, too, and there was no way he ever earned more than a couple of event ribbons at school during the annual National Youth Games. The difference was: he had not only graduated from school (I had too, mind you) but also stuck around for another couple of years and then spent a few years doing his medical specialization and was now an esteemed member of the academic clique that, in my view, had always been the other part of the world's population, the middle class. By contrast, I had dropped out of school because the guy I was doing my vocational apprenticeship under kept pissing me off, and the apprentice-level pay (that expression alone makes clear that we're not really talking about money but at most alms) wasn't anywhere near enough for my basic monthly alcohol and drug consumption—to say nothing of duds, wheels, and girl-related outlays.

Somehow I found myself on the verge of falling back into the schmaltz again. First the compassion routine with the dead girl, now regret about screwing up my career track—maybe I was on some path of knowledge, with atonement waiting for me at its end, and then paradise? I pulled myself together, forced myself away from the screen, and started looking for Martin.

I lucked out in the break room. Standing next to Martin were Katrin and their colleague Jochen (the guy with the old city maps), along with a man in a suit and tie, who I already knew was the boss and who was noisily slurping some steamy liquid. They were chatting about their upcoming move. *Move???*

My heart sank to my boots, figuratively speaking. That whole wing of the building was going to be cleared out. Only the bodies would still be lying alone in their morgue drawers, all life was going to be removed, to live on somewhere else. Here would dwell death, and it alone. The employees would stop by to do their autopsies, and they'd wash their hands and disappear. I felt like bawling yet again. Today was definitely not my day. I perched on Katrin's shoulder, imagining being able to feel her satiny hair and touch her silky skin, and I gradually calmed back down. Slowly but surely, I started trying to establish contact with her. I whispered "Katrin" and "Kitty" and things like that, focusing my imagination on her hot high beams and blazing chassis and sending her a fiery look from my eyes and hot breath from my mouth, which I blew into the neckline of her tight-fitting sweater. I mumbled a whole litany of dirty comments into her ear, imagining her naked skin and quivering body materializing before me.

Nothing. No reaction. I was getting pretty tired of the whole thing, myself, because of course nothing was getting excited on my end, either. I was overcome with the memory of a time when my face was covered in zits and I had to regularly change my pajamas—and it wasn't because of ring around the collar, if you know what I mean. Yet another maudlin tailspin into deep, emotional darkness.

Now I'd had enough. I hadn't suffered as much as I had today for a very long time. If this was the road to paradise, then to hell with it.

"Martin," I yelled, and he winced as expected. "Can we please talk about continuing my investigation now?"

He mumbled "excuse me" to the others and hastily left the break room. I followed him but not without quickly blowing Katrin one more imaginary kiss.

We had hardly stepped out of the break room when I asked, "Who killed her?" Martin was moving toward his office.

"No one," he said, rushing down the corridor. I don't know why he was in such a hurry, but I had no problem following him.

"Are you trying to bullshit me?" I asked less than obligingly, but I apologized immediately to avoid putting Martin's willingness to cooperate to too hard a test.

"She died of anaphylactic shock."

"I see." My basic understanding of medicine consists of a fairly narrow list of topics. Colds, headaches, the runs, withdrawal, things like that. "Anaphylactic shock" doesn't rank among them, as I'm sure you've already surmised. Martin apparently couldn't conceive of someone having so large a knowledge gap because only after multiple inquiries did he deign to tell me the woman had kicked the bucket from an allergy. Up to that point I had always thought people with allergies were posers. They're not actually sick, properly speaking, but they have a totally exaggerated response to things that to normal people are just normal things. Like pollen. Or hazelnuts, as in the case of the body under discussion here. It was news to me that someone could die from such a made-up-sounding story. It was presumably news to that woman, too, although her advance in knowledge couldn't have lasted long since it was interrupted—indeed, ended—by her abrupt death. Shit happens, you might now say, and that would describe her manner of death quite aptly. However, the cause of her early demise did pose one compelling question.

"Why in the hell does someone try to get rid of a body that died from a hazelnut?"

Martin shrugged.

"Are you sure someone didn't actually coax her along?" I probed.

"Of course, the chemical toxicology results have not come in yet."

For once I understood his answer right away—and was somehow proud of that.

"But, by and large, I am sure, yes."

Neither of us said anything for a little while. Martin stared at his screen.

"OK, don't make me squeeze every word out individually," I said, repeating the exact words my mother used to say to piss me off.

"She is approximately in her mid-twenties, height one hundred fifty-two centimeters, and weight forty-two kilograms. At the time of her death she was fairly healthy, apart from a slight cold. She had taken a nonprescription over-the-counter medicine for the cold. In addition, her last meal consisted of cookies with hazelnuts."

"Hmm."

"Her teeth had been subject to dental efforts that fall short of German standards."

My God, sometimes he expressed himself in such a ridiculously complicated way.

"And shortly before her death she had sexual intercourse." Ah ha, now we were getting to the interesting bits.

"Who with?" I immediately asked, naturally, since that is one of the most important sex-related questions. Who did it with who?

"No idea," Martin answered.

"No DNA?" I replied, because of course any kid knows that they can convict sex offenders nowadays using the DNA evidence they leave behind. You know, sperm and all that.

"There is also DNA evidence," Martin lectured. "But it has not been evaluated yet."

We didn't say anything for a while again.

"There is pubic hair that did not originate from her. Dermal abrasions on her heels, which were presumably sustained while being carried to the vehicle. Further abrasions dorsally, presumably caused by the carpeting in the trunk. Some abrasions at sites where she was presumably touched by the perpetrator as she was packed into the vehicle. And a whole list of additional fibers and all kinds of marks that stem from the location where the body was discarded."

"Where was that actually?" I asked. "Where did they find her?"

"At the sewage plant."

I sensed Martin wondering whether it had mattered to her at all to have been in such a place. Right after these thoughts unintentionally whizzed through his brain came this next thought: That's complete nonsense. The woman is dead; she couldn't have been aware of where they discarded her. And then: But Pascha is aware of everything. Martin resisted these thoughts, but they could not be driven out; they came crashing in on him, pestering him, I could sense it exactly. He shook his head, but that didn't help, of course. Good old Martin was well on his way toward an authentic, full-on breakdown.

"Have you, um, are you able to . . . sense anything with her?" he stammered.

"No, man, the woman's dead as a doornail," I said, hoping my clear language would make him feel better. It didn't work. He winced as though someone had made an unseemly comment about a third party, only to find that person had overheard the whole thing.

"Have you ever given any thought to something like that before?" I asked.

"Of course not," Martin replied.

"All right then," I said. "So you should leave it at that. I'm just some kind of cosmic accident, and all the others are dead, all right?"

He nodded but didn't seem convinced.

"I think I'll head back home then," he said.

I sighed. I had actually been hoping he would still come up with another couple of interesting findings today, but

Martin was definitely in no position to be formulating even one more lucid thought or listening to me lay out my still-incomplete, although brilliant, theories.

"Do you think you could turn on the TV in Conference Room Two for me?" I asked. He nodded, grabbed his coat, turned on the TV, and drove home.

———

"A condom was not used. But lubricant was," Martin reported the next morning.

A hooker. Holy hang-gliding whores, that woman was a pro! And, holy crowing cocks, Martin was like a new man this morning. He'd already taken his coat off and swung open the door to the conference room so vigorously it almost damaged the wall. I winced, as I sat in front of a morning talk show.

"Are you here?" he asked carefully. "You're not saying anything."

"I'm here and can tell you what the current national weather conditions are right now, what today's forecast is, and how many calories a butter croissant without butter has."

He didn't seem to know what to do with that answer for a second. Then he stared at the screen. The repugnantly upbeat talking head with the artificially tousled hair and a smile paralyzed by too much cosmetic surgery was just explaining what should be part of a really healthy break-fast: muesli, minus the sugar, soaked in hot water and then rinsed down with a glass of freshly squeezed fruit juice. Personally, if I had still had the choice, I wouldn't chase pap like that with a glass of juice; instead, I'd blast it down the pipes with a high-energy surge from the toilet tank, but on this point tastes do indeed diverge just a bit.

"Good. The report is complete; should we go through it once?" Martin suggested a bit abruptly.

The gentleman was offering me his cooperation on a silver tray? Yes; so what was the deal with him today? Had he resorted to taking drugs? Smoking, swallowing, shooting up? I resolved not to inquire further but just play along.

"I'd love to, Martin. Great."

I sounded like a social worker reciting a standard de-escalation script in response to insults or death threats, as blasé as if I'd been asked what time it was. Outwardly casual and friendly, but artificial like a Christmas tree in Abu Dhabi.

"There is still no clue to her identity," Martin lectured, "apart from the quality of the dental work, which presumably points to Eastern Europe."

"I see," I said.

They call that "active listening" when you keep mumbling things like "hmm" and "uh-huh" and "you don't say" now and again. I learned that on TV, at five forty-five, when they run the "Be Your Own Ghostwriter" segment on effective communication in today's world.

"Her overall health status was fairly good, but she was perhaps a bit underweight."

"Uh-huh."

An irreproachable effective-communication strategy: I swallowed my objection that she was unable to benefit from good health anymore as she now, unfortunately, and despite an excellent constitution, was dead, because Martin might have taken that as a provocation. So, I just said "uh-huh."

"There were some fibers under her fingernails that could have come from an expensive wool carpet."

"Hmm."

At the next rhetorical pause I would have to start over with "I see" to keep applying my effective-communication skills, but it didn't come to that.

"Overall we can say that the woman died a natural death, which the person who intended the body to disappear either did not realize or did realize, but nevertheless did not wish to follow the prescribed procedure for reporting a death, with the issuance of an official death certificate."

"What conclusion can we draw from this?" I asked carefully, using the word "we" intentionally to solidify Martin's sudden engagement and to clearly signal solidarity on my end.

"She was not murdered, so there is no murderer."

"How does that help us?" I asked, since I couldn't really follow Martin's train of thought.

"Since there is no murderer who killed the young woman, there is also no reason to kill you, because you did not discover a murder when you saw the woman in the trunk."

My standard rhetorical script stuck in my throat. So that's why Martin was in such a good mood. He had discovered that the guy he thought was the woman's murderer wasn't a murderer at all, and so all was right with the world again. There was just one snag.

"But someone did kill me, Martin!"

The self-control I had laboriously drilled into myself was now down the tubes; my response to this unbelievably stupid finding by my only possible earthbound assistant was no longer informed by morning television for the rhetorically self-righteous but instead by the action flicks I had taken in between ten last night and two this morning.

"Somebody, whether it was the guy who stowed that chick in the trunk or somebody else, KILLED me! I couldn't care less if some underweight babe kicked it because she ate some nut or a blue bean, for that matter."

Martin gasped for air, but I wasn't done yet.

"Maybe the guy who put her in the trunk didn't kill her, but we still totally know for absolutely sure that he didn't want to be connected to the dead Jane Doe. So he wanted to get rid of her. So he might not have been particularly happy that somebody, namely the guy who stole his car, suddenly found out that he had a dead woman in his trunk. So, it may have occurred to him to push the little car thief off the bridge."

Martin was getting paler and paler, and now he looked just as unhappy as he had last night.

"But you don't know whose car you stole, do you?"

"No," I replied. "But the other guy doesn't know that, either."

Martin collapsed into one of the conference chairs, completely exhausted. "So what do we do now?" he asked.

"We've got to find out who the b . . ." I quickly swallowed the word "bitch" and continued, ". . . who the body is."

Martin looked at me admonishingly, maybe he sensed the word before I changed my phrasing.

"The police are responsible for that," he said.

"The police won't be able to figure anything out, the way things work in their world," I said.

"In 'their' world?" Martin asked.

Ugh, again with the slow uptake that keeps pissing me off.

"OK, the woman has been dead for eight days, right?" I asked.

He nodded.

"And she hasn't been reported missing yet, right?"

Nodding.

"And she's got Eastern European choppers and is presumably a pro?"

More nodding.

"Do you think she's been staying in Germany legally?" Now he'd finally gotten it!

"But . . ." he began. But I definitively refused to entertain any further protest.

"People in the real world do not think you're a cop," I said. The mere idea that Mr. Roly-Poly Blunderhead here could be a member of a law enforcement agency was a complete joke. "You've got a chance to find out her identity."

"But what should I say about why I'm looking for her?"

If I'd had eyes, I'd have rolled them up so high they spun through my head twice.

"Just say that you fell in love with her," I joked.

Martin took the suggestion seriously. "But then I would need to know her name," he objected.

"You could have seen her waiting in line at the grocery store and immediately fallen head over heels for her," I said, spinning the web tighter. Just like in those romantic comedies they run on cable between three and five in the morning for the sentimental and sleepless. Even though I was making fun of him, I recognized it was a terrific idea. Martin would play the unhappy-in-love guy with absolute credibility. He came off as harmless and inspired pity. If he couldn't get any information about the woman using that whole shtick, then nothing and no one could uncover her identity. Bingo!

In his thoughts he was still coming up with objections, such as the fact that the police were surely still looking into her identity, and he didn't want to get in those guys' way, but he didn't protest anymore. After all, it'd also occurred to him that the cops didn't have the slightest inkling where to starting looking for the woman's identity. They also didn't know she'd been stuck into the car, which they also didn't even know I had stolen. And, again, Martin couldn't just clue all his detective buddies in on these facts, since then he'd have to explain how he came to know it all . . . Instead he completely gave up his mental protests and accepted that the search for the woman's identity would have to depend on him.

However, another small problem just occurred to me. If the guy who fell for the hottie at the grocery store checkout were now to go running around with a photo of her dead body, then our oh-so-sappy story might have a tiny credibility problem. But Martin just thought:

"No problem. For cases like this we use some software that generates a drawing from a photo."

Well then, that should do.

After a night of television terror and morning of grueling discussion, I wanted to enjoy a few quiet hours to myself, so I floated down to the autopsy section, fluttered past the autopsy room without looking inside, and slid into Morgue Drawer Four.

I noticed it right away: something was not right. I didn't feel at home. I felt like I was in a grave. I felt defiled, in a really disgusting way. I was surprised at myself. One's own body shouldn't actually trigger feelings of disgust, especially since it had been washed clean—which during my lifetime had not always been the case. But, anyways, I was strangely affected by myself and considered what I would do when the drawer pulled open. A lightbulb flashed on, and then came the blow: there was a strange body in Morgue Drawer Four! And specifically a rather, no, not rather, but a very, very disgusting one! I'll spare you the details, but the body wasn't that fresh anymore, if you get my drift. It was swollen up, discolored, and featured an injury to the skull that was presumably caused by an ax or log-splitting maul. I'm quoting the autopsy report here, which was to be dictated at the then-pending postmortem, so at least I don't have to describe the grizzly zombie face in my own words. And to think I was lying on top of a body like that. Laid myself to rest. At first I felt really sick to my stomach, although without a stomach and the accompanying neurons that was no longer possible, but if I could have, I would have puked the whole morgue drawer full. Just like that. Virtually.

But next I was hit by something else, namely this realization: my body was gone! It had been lying in Morgue Drawer Four since I had been pushed off the overpass bridge, and now it was gone. Where was I?

I raced over to Martin, ambushed him from out of the darkness and yelled, "Where is my body?"

Martin winced, gathered his thoughts that had been immersed in a report, and absently mumbled, "The district attorney's office released it, and it was subsequently picked up by a mortician."

"A mortician?" I asked as though I didn't know what that is.

"Yes, by a mortician. To prepare it for the burial."

The word floored me. Burial. My body was being taken away from me. My morgue drawer. My home. My last known address: Institute for Forensic Medicine, Morgue Drawer 4. I was homeless.

I was speechless. Martin had dived with his thoughts deep back into his report and wasn't paying attention to me at all. And so it begins, I thought to myself. You're losing your home, you're hardly perceptible, and at some point you'll be all gone. No one will remember you anymore, no one will talk to you anymore. I disappeared off into the break room, perched on top of the coffee machine, and even among all of these people coming and going and drinking coffee I felt lonely and sorry for myself.

The closer it got to quitting time, the more nervous Martin got. Initially it seemed like he was having trouble with his stupid headset; he kept joggling it around and taking it off to massage the spot over his left ear where the earpiece had already pressed an authentic dent into his skull, and he kept repositioning the cord connecting the headset to his computer about a thousand times a minute. I didn't want to harp on him about it, but if he could just type the report like a normal person he'd probably have had an easier time. Anyways, it may well be that his imminent deployment as a lovesick grocery store customer was also notching up his nervousness. Then when I asked if he'd had the photograph converted, his self-control fizzled like a fart on fire.

"That's actually really hard for me to get done as long as my colleagues can tell on the system that I'm online," he snarled at me.

"How so? You can just say that it's for your collection of hot-babe photos," I replied, and he gasped for air. Martin was opening and closing his mouth like a dying fish, and he was turning bright red to boot. The colleague seated across looked up at him in alarm.

"Are you choking?" he asked.

Martin nodded, coughed, breathed frantically, and suddenly stood up waving his colleague off when he wanted to follow Martin and help, and then he headed to the bathroom. I slowly followed, even though I wasn't really able to help. I started getting worried. How was my sweet Little Goose going to start an investigation among illegal immigrants, drug dealers, and hookers if he suffered respiratory arrest from even a tiny, harmless bit of fun? Would an undocumented Eastern European deign give him mouth-to-mouth if that happened to him right in the middle of a Russian nightclub? And in that case, would that person then infect Martin with an active case of pulmonary tuberculosis? I'd heard a few things along those lines in the last few days.

———•———

Martin calmed back down, and the color of his face had returned to its usual office grey, and after seizing the moment and taking a piss, he leaned against the wall breathing heavily.

"Sorry," I mumbled.

He just nodded.

"I didn't mean it that way," I added.

"It's fine," he squeezed out. "I just have to get used to the fact that you are unfamiliar with either compassion or good manners. You claim that I'm the one with a perverse profession, yet you show absolutely no respect for the dead."

I wanted to answer, but he waved me away and opened the door.

"Nor for the living."

Strong exit. Or at least, it would have been, if he had zipped up his pants again.

———•———

We had apparently signed some kind of armistice as we got on our way. Where exactly we were going I don't want to explain in further detail here, because I am respecting the desire for anonymity so cherished by the group we intended to question, for obvious reasons. Nicely phrased, right?

I didn't make any more jokes and didn't mention his open fly, and he didn't actually say anything at all. Anyways, he'd fed the head shot of the dead girl through the drawing program without being caught; he touched it up a bit and ended up with a pretty good, alive-seeming sketch of her.

———•———

We climbed into the trash can, whose side window was still broken, and left the well-lit streets of the middle-class areas of town behind us. Martin carefully locked up the car, and

I kept my trap shut. He looked around, unsure, feeling not at all at ease in his skin, checked one more time that he had the paper with the drawing of the woman in his pocket, and set out. I stayed in the vicinity of his left shoulder, but I kept looking in all directions.

"So far so good," I whispered to calm him down.

He approached a group of six boys who were standing together smoking, gawking up and down the street.

"Excuse me, um, good evening," Martin said. The six of them were now gawking at him.

"I have a question for you," Martin said politely.

Still no reaction. I looked around, everything quiet.

"I'm looking for a woman," he said, fumbling in his pocket for the drawing.

"To fuck," one of the boys said, and the others laughed.

"No, no," Martin quickly corrected himself. "I met her and would like to see her again."

"But not fuck her?" the guy asked again. "What else is a woman for?"

Martin had unfolded the drawing and was showing it to them. One of the boys grabbed his balls when he saw the drawing and moaned loudly. The others laughed again.

"Do you happen to know her name?" Martin politely asked.

"You met her and don't know her name?" the spokesman said. "What did the two of you do, then?"

The roars were growing louder. Counter to my fears, Martin stayed pretty cool. He was pretending the sleazy comments weren't even reaching him, although I could sense the waves of disgust emanating from his direction.

If he found my little jokes disrespectful, then he must be pretty close to puking here.

"I'll take you to her," the ringleader said. "Give me a hundred, and I'll take you to her right away."

I didn't need to make a sound; the red warning light in Martin's brain had started flashing all on its own.

"Is she here right now?" Martin asked after a millisecond, during which I was afraid he'd start screaming out loud.

"Of course."

Somehow the situation was slowly getting absurd. We were looking for a woman we knew was in the freezer at the Institute, and this guy is telling us he'll take us to her. Now how to explain we knew he was bullshitting us when you weren't allowed to say what you knew? But Martin had a great idea.

"Could you check?" Martin asked. "Just give her a call."

"She's around here," the guy replied, standing up to his full height. "Why, don't you believe me?"

The menacing tone of the last question was not appealing to either of us, but Martin admittedly had the disadvantage of being vulnerable to attack if it came to that. He winced on the inside but then pulled himself together and stayed really casual on the outside. For Martin, I mean. Under his duffle coat you couldn't discern much of his shivering, fortunately.

"I don't have a hundred euros on me," Martin said. "So it'd be easier for you just to call her. Then she can tell me if she wants to see me or not."

"Phone calls are so impersonal," the guy said.

The others were standing closer together, and an intangible but still-appreciable aggressiveness was in the air.

"Please give me the picture back," Martin said. "I don't think this is heading anywhere."

"We're not heading anywhere because you don't want to come with us. We want to help you," the spokesman murmured.

I almost puked. When guys like this say, "we want to help you, man" in a tone like that, then you should really get far, far away really, really fast. The help they mean is usually not of the type that one might wish for. Or do you think full blows to both sides of the head at the same time are very helpful? Occasionally their objective is only to "drive bad thoughts out of your mind," but usually it drives only one thing—namely, a hole into your eardrum.

"Thank you, but I'd prefer not to burst in somewhere unannounced," Martin said, taking two steps to the side and walking past the boys on his trembling legs. "You can keep the drawing, if you'd like."

We kept walking, and I looked behind us again. The boys had crumpled the drawing up into a little ball and were swatting it back and forth to each other like a beanie bag. One of them was talking in a language I didn't understand, and the rest of them gave loud and dirty laughs. In the end they didn't seem to want to pick a fight beyond taking the picture. I was relieved and informed Martin of my observations. He was also slowly exhaling all the air he had taken from fear as the boys were cackling.

He found his tongue again amazingly fast, and then I quickly got what was coming to me.

"I feel really no particular inclination to serve as the strange object of amusement again for interviewees with testosterone swamping every sulcus of their brains."

Which in simple words meant: He's scared shitless of gorillas. And he's right.

"I'm sure that sooner or later the detectives will figure out the name and address of the woman by their own means, and they can then conduct the further investigation," he grumbled at no one in particular. His blind faith in the abilities of the criminal investigation unit did him credit of course, but they also showed how little a clue he actually had. Because the investigators are not the ones who control the discovery of information like that: folks on the street do. And as far as the willingness to cooperate goes on the part of boneheads like the aforesaid testosterone junkies, Martin was actually going to need someone to clue him in at some point. But right now didn't seem like the best time.

"There is always somebody who comes forward with a helpful piece of information," Martin said. He was starting to sound like a defiant little brat who starts every sentence with "but I want . . ."

"And when will that be happening?" I asked him. "Next millennium? When the little green men start landing here? By then the worms will have eaten their fill and be relaxing on my bones, burping, and there won't be even one bastard around anymore who gives a rat's ass that the bitch that your computer blurred up a pretty picture of may have been the reason that some small-time car thief got pushed off the bridge."

I shouldn't have said the word "bitch." It just slipped out; in the lingo of my world it doesn't imply anything negative, either. It just means "woman." But Martin didn't know that; he of course speaks only his silted academese, so now I had a real problem. I noticed it the millisecond I said it. Martin was closing the game down. And not just that, he turned around and started walking back to his car. Not a good idea.

"Martin, I'm sorry. I didn't mean to say that, I didn't mean it that way; the people who I hang out with just say 'bitch' and don't mean it in a bad way, but please don't walk back past those big guys."

It seemed like he didn't hear me at all, but the big guys did seem to see him. One of them, anyways. He stood up and watched the little roly-poly man in the little wool coat approach his boys in their T-shirts.

"Martin, wake up and turn around!" I yelled. "Let's talk about it again, I'll apologize again, a hundred more times, no problem, but turn around now and get scarce before those bruisers up there decide your curiosity is pissing them off more than they let on before."

He pretended not to hear me at all.

"Goddamnit, Martin, they'll punch your nose in so flat you'll only be able to breathe the thin air at two thousand meters."

No response, even though I'd made an extra effort to imbue my warning with a scientific touch.

"Plus you'll puke, piss blood, and you'll spend your next twelve paychecks on the dentist."

He hesitated, but now he'd come too close to them again. Meanwhile, four of the big boys had turned around and were watching him. Martin kept staring at the ground in front of him. I sensed that he was slowly panicking.

"Take off!" I yelled again. "Now!"

Martin bent over, reached into the dirt with his right hand, stood up again, mumbled a friendly "There's my button!" toward the big boys, turned around, and started breathing again. Shallow and fast, but even so . . . air in, air out, that's all you can do when you're in utter panic to keep your lungs from sticking shut like a vacuum-sealed freezer bag.

With trembling knees, Martin walked the same path again that he had covered two minutes ago. This time it was a physical or psychological or whatever kind of wonder that he was able to move like this at all.

So right at the outset of our investigation we'd had bad luck. Unfriendly types like that, as Martin would presumably call those glistening assholes, were everywhere, but they're not necessarily the biggest group, just the loudest. To get to the point, as the evening went on the level of aggression abated. But it didn't get much easier for Martin because our next encounter was with a professional streetwalker.

"Good evening," Martin said cheerfully.

I was already smiling before he said anything else.

"Hey, sweet ting, what I can do for you?" the woman asked, her face hardly visible in the darkness. At the time I thought not being able to see her was a small mercy, and I still do now. Her accent was so thick you had to think for a second to decide whether she was speaking German at all. Plus, she was reeling off the words like she'd learned them by heart. Which is probably true. How many sentences does a hooker actually need for her business model? Four? Five? I guess we were about to find out.

"I'm looking for a woman," Martin said, and, as you probably expected, this phrasing of course gave rise to an eensy-weensie misunderstanding in this context.

"You fount woman, sweet ting," the woman cooed.

This unexpected answer threw Martin a little, so he did a double-take and took a closer look at the woman than he had at first. His slightly disbelieving eyes wandered down, scrutinizing her clothes with increasing bewilderment. "Clothes" is of course a bit overstated. Here in winter she was wearing a slightly threadbare, faux-fur spaghetti-strap crop-top that gave the impression she was suckling a mangy animal, paired with some kind of overstretched wrist-warmer she wore where an upstanding lady would have worn a skirt. The most generously sized attire she had on was her boots, which came up over her knees. But the thin leather cracking off in several spots undoubtedly didn't have that high of a thermal rating, either.

"Say, aren't you cold?" Martin asked abruptly.

"You want warm me up?" she cooed.

"Um . . ." Martin said, cutting himself short. Obviously he didn't want to warm her up, but he didn't want to be impolite and just say no, either. It's hard out here for a gentleman!

He pulled out another copy of the drawing from his pocket and held it out for the lady to see.

"I'm looking for this woman."

"I can for you be any woman of worlt. Girlfrient, teacher, mama, whatever you wanting."

Either this lady had frequent interactions in her line of work with men for whom she was supposed to play a certain role, or her German was much better than I had expected.

"No, you've misunderstood," Martin explained, undaunted. "I'm looking for *this* woman. Do you know her?"

She blinked at the drawing, reached for it, and held it about two centimeters from her pupils. Blind as a bat. That might be an advantage in her line of work, I thought to myself. In the end not every trick who's into whores with black boots are as nice as Richard Gere.

"No," she said, returning the paper. "You come with me."

"I'm looking only for this woman; it's very important," Martin said, looking as sad as a dog into whose bowl you've sliced a piece of tofu sausage.

"Sorry," the woman said, and it sounded like she meant it. "Goot luck." And with that the matter was closed.

Martin stuck the drawing back into his pocket, thanked her again politely, and walked on.

"How can she stand the cold like that, half-naked?" he asked me.

On that point of course he was asking the wrong guy, because I've never understood women's response to temperature. The second you're nice and warm under the covers, they slide their ice-cold feet over onto your calves, and presumably after holding an ice cube for the five hours before bedtime they lay their hands on your stomach. But if you then even remotely flinch, they start griping that men just cannot cuddle. Newsflash: men can cuddle. They even want to. Just not with ice cubes.

On the other hand, women will walk around in the depths of winter with bare midriffs and short skirts and ridiculous contrivances they call "shoes" when there are ice and snow on the street, and they fight tooth and nail against socks, warm jackets, or—God forbid—stocking caps. It doesn't make any difference to me if women want to freeze themselves to death, but in the end they always come down with a bladder infection, and then you're stuck another week without sex. A basic grasp of preventive medicine is such an easy thing to pick up, and you don't even have to go to school to learn it, but somehow girls just do not get how it all works.

Martin and I each dwelled briefly on our thoughts, and then we looked for other victims to interrogate. We found them at news kiosks, game halls—although Martin displayed a certain Pavlovian timidity entering gambling establishments for the ordinary man—at street food stands, restaurants, pubs, bars, and the bouncer in front of a night-club. The conversations were all more or less the same, apart from one that stood out from the rest.

It was with the aforesaid nightclub bouncer who Martin showed the drawing to. There were clear traces of advancing fatigue in Martin's face.

"I'm not a credit-rating agency, Buddy," said the Black Giant, whose smooth-shaven skull was a sparkly slime-green because it was reflecting the light from the club's neon sign.

When men taller than 190 or shorter than 170 centimeters call you "Buddy," incidentally, there is call for increased caution, which is why all of my warning lights immediately started flashing.

"I really hate to bother you with a favor, but I've got to know what her name is and where she lives," Martin said. You could hear clear exhaustion and a certain resignation that had set in his voice. The only way I'd been able to convince him to keep going at all was with maximum effort and urgency. So this guy here was going to be our last witness.

"What are you looking for her for, Buddy?" the Black Giant asked.

Over the course of the evening I'd determined that my position as disinterested observer entailed unexpected advantages. Up to this point my immateriality was an "extreme burden" on me, as a shrink would presumably say. But my unobservability had also had its advantages during the countless conversations Martin had had all night. I was free to pay much closer attention to what people were saying between the lines. Usually there wasn't much there, other than angling how to trade a piece of information for money.

But as Martin was rattling off his story about the girl from the grocery store checkout line, my warning bells suddenly went off. The bouncer wasn't making a particularly affable impression, but he wasn't really acting like a thug, either. Still, his vibe had something menacing about it, and I had the impression the guy knew more than what he was telling us.

"Martin," I called. "This guy knows something."

Martin responded promptly.

"Are you sure you haven't seen this woman even once?" he asked politely. "It's really incredibly important to me."

"When I say no, that applies to the first, second, and third time you ask the same question," the bouncer said. He was parleying as though he'd been a humanities major. And maybe he was. There are barkeeps with PhDs and taxi drivers with tenure at the university, after all!

"She may not speak German," Martin said, as though he hadn't heard the objection.

The Black Giant didn't say anything.

"I'm sure that you know more than you want to tell me," Martin said, politely.

"And I'm sure that you'd better get scarce," the bouncer replied, sounding not at all amicable.

"All right, we're done for tonight," I said.

"Well, thank you very much for your time," Martin said, turning around. He stuck the drawing, which the bouncer had taken a curious look at but not touched, back into his duffle coat pocket as he snuck down the dark alley toward the car.

"No matter what he knows, he'd never have said anything in a hundred years," I said, trying to console him. The way Martin had to be trotting along here at one thirty in the morning, you really had to feel sorry for him.

"Hmm," he muttered.

I think he was just wiped out.

His car hadn't been damaged any further, which didn't surprise me because most people have a kind of amused affection for a 2CV, no matter what kind of crowd you hang out in.

Martin was driving so carefully, but to make matters worse he still got flagged into a drunk-driving checkpoint. In response to the question whether he had drunk any alcohol, he said no; in response to the question where was he coming from and where had he spent the whole evening and half of the night, he stated he was looking for his girlfriend. Was she missing? No. Uh-huh. She had run off with a guy, Martin explained. This statement in conjunction with the dark rings under his anguished-looking eyes redeemed him, and the police were nice enough to wish him well and good luck with his girlfriend. Martin was slowly but surely evolving into a skilled liar. But there was no way my praise could coax even one more grunt out of him tonight.

Once home, he crashed still-dressed into his bed and immediately fell asleep. Oh, fabulous! Now I could take a look at his collection of city maps in peace. I've always *dreamed* of something like this. I looked over at the TV and determined that Meticulous Martin didn't leave the set in standby mode because standby still draws too much electricity, so I had to marinate in my bad mood until morning.

Morning started rather early, when someone began incessantly ringing the doorbell at seven. The noise pierced through me down to my balls, because it took a solid three minutes for Martin to emerge from the bedroom. He looked like an animal had eaten him, half-digested him, and hacked him back up again.

It was Gregor, Martin's detective friend. At seven in the morning. Just guess if he came as a friend or as a detective. Exactly, criminal investigation.

"Didn't sleep much last night, eh?" he said, greeting Martin and heading right into the kitchen. "Coffee?"

Martin mumbled something incomprehensible and vanished into the bathroom. Gregor putzed around in the kitchen. I decided to go into the kitchen, too. Watching people in the bathroom in the morning is not really my thing. Plus, I wanted to know what had brought Gregor over here so early in the morning.

Gregor found a can of coffee beans, grabbed the grinder, and started turning the crank. By hand. Have you ever seen such a thing? He did it without any kind of amazement, but since he apparently knew his way around his friend's place pretty well, he apparently also knew how pointless it would be to look for instant. Anyone who normally sips tea from the finest porcelain would likewise turn the guzzling of coffee into some kind of fussy, civilized ceremony. So Gregor was endeavoring to prepare a cultivated coffee and had just finish brewing when Martin entered the kitchen, freshly showered but still far from top form. He took the mug that Gregor handed him with a mumbled thank-you. Then, totally exhausted, he collapsed onto one of the two stools that were half-slid under the breakfast table the size of a proper gentleman's handkerchief.

"An all-night investigation like that is pretty tiring, huh?" Gregor said.

Martin nodded, staring at his coffee while Gregor added fresh milk and a half spoon of sugar for him. Man, I'd never have expected so much mothering from a heavyset criminal investigator. But apparently Gregor was playing the good cop/bad cop routine here in one person. The good one had made the coffee; the bad one was going to continue his questioning.

"It's especially tiring when you have to watch your back loitering around the roughest corners of the city all night while still doing a professional job looking around. Right?"

Martin nodded again.

"So you see why police officers always go in pairs."

No one said anything for a while, interrupted occasionally by Gregor sipping his coffee. Martin drank silently.

"So, what the hell is going on?" Gregor asked once he'd had enough of the mutual silence.

"I wanted to find out who the dead Jane Doe is," Martin said.

Of course that wasn't particularly helpful since Gregor evidently already knew that; otherwise he wouldn't have been standing around all healthy, wealthy, and wise here in Martin's kitchen instead of at home in his own warm bed.

"Your great love from the grocery store," he said, caustically. "God, Martin. I'm serious," he then added, now no longer looking irritated but really very, very serious. "You have put yourself and me into an impossible situation."

"How do you know anything about it?" Martin asked.

"Let's just say there are people who hang out in ugly crowds even though they may not be that ugly themselves," Gregor said. "Some of them are also happy to pass on a tip now and then when something strange crops up."

"The bouncer," I yelled.

"The bouncer," Martin said.

"Yes, the bouncer," Gregor said.

If all morning meetings were going to be of this caliber, they really should ban office hours before nine a.m., I thought, but out of caution I didn't say anything.

"What is your relationship to that woman?" Gregor asked.

"I, um, well . . ."

We weren't getting anywhere like this. "Tell him the whole truth," I suggested.

Martin's cerebral convolutions were slowly warming up, but for the life of him he couldn't come up with an even semiplausible reason for his nocturnal outing to the rough side of town. So he sighed loudly once, breathed deeply, and laid it all out.

"Nine days ago, that woman was lying in the trunk of a Mercedes SLR that was stolen that same day by Sascha Lerchenberg."

Gregor stared at him and, as he wasn't paying attention to his cup anymore, poured a generous quantity of coffee onto his pants. His scream sounded a bit exaggerated to my ears, but as we all know the male of the species is apparently hypersensitive to temperature. Martin responded as a doctor immediately, jumping up and filling a cup from the drainer with cold water and pouring it with skillful speed onto Gregor's pants. He screamed again. Then he grabbed a kitchen towel, groping himself and rubbing, and he disappeared briefly into the bathroom to return without pants, wrapped in a towel. Fortunately he didn't wear a uniform jacket since he was a detective; otherwise my ensuing laughing fit would have scattered my molecules to kingdom come. Although I quickly regained my composure, Martin remained totally listless; he didn't smile even once. Poor Little Goose.

"You just mentioned Sascha Lerchenberg," Gregor said, resuming the thread of the conversation as though nothing had happened. "That's the guy who fell off the temporary bridge at the transit hub, right?"

"He was pushed," Martin said, without my having to remind him. Very good.

"The report said there wasn't any evidence of a push," Gregor said.

"And there isn't," Martin said. "But he told me."

Short pause.

"Who?" Gregor asked.

"Pascha."

Longer pause.

Gregor: "Who is Pascha?"

Martin: "That's the name Sascha went by."

Gregor: "And he told you this?"

Martin: "Exactly."

Gregor: "When?"

Martin: "Shortly after the postmortem."

Unpleasantly long pause.

Gregor: "You mean, after you cut up his body, removed all the organs and preserved a small piece of each, stuffed everything back into the abdominal cavity, and then sutured him back up again?"

Martin: "Exactly. His spirit isn't dead. He can't find peace. He's been buzzing around us down in the morgue." Rather long pause.

Gregor: "And he talks to you?"

Martin: "Exactly."

Very long pause. Martin took a microsip of his coffee again, presumably so he could nurse the one mugful through the whole morning, or at least as long as this interrogation lasted. I waited with quasi-bated breath for Gregor's reaction. We could only assume the worst based on his expression; to my boundless regret I couldn't find any way into the convolutions of his brain.

"Do other dead people talk to you?" Gregor asked.

Martin shook his head.

"Can your colleagues hear this Pascha, too?"

"No, I'm the only one he can contact."

"And he told you that you're supposed to find out the identity of this woman?"

Martin nodded.

"Why?"

Martin sighed. "He wants me to find out who pushed him. I couldn't exactly include in my report that he told me he was pushed. And the connection to that woman's body in the trunk and all of that—there was no way for me to have known that, and so I didn't tell you anything about it either, because then I'd have to tell you about him—and there's absolutely no one who would believe me. Right?"

Martin looked into Gregor's eyes for the first time. Now Gregor was the one who looked away.

"That's what I thought," Martin said. "Two weeks ago I wouldn't have believed it myself."

Neither of them said anything again for a while, and then Gregor went back into the bathroom, got dressed, came back out, and sat next to Martin at the table.

"You should take some time off," he told Martin. Martin shook his head.

"Then at least take today off."

"I'm off this morning," Martin said. "But this afternoon I'm on duty."

Gregor stood up and explained to Martin in a rather official voice that he should please refrain from investigating dead Jane Does since he was interfering with the detectives' investigation, and then Gregor said goodbye in his friendly voice again, and left. Martin looked at the clock, ran his fingers through his still-damp hair, and stood up.

"We've got to get going," he said.

"Where to?" I asked Martin.

"To your funeral."

FIVE

The moment I had secretly been scared stiff of the whole time had finally arrived: my funeral. Naturally, I hadn't anticipated attending it. Well, that is, I hadn't anticipated *naturally* attending it. My body was the main attraction, you know. I had successfully suppressed any thought that I, that is, my own consciousness, would watch myself be buried. Suppression was now a thing of the past.

"Do we have to?" I asked Martin.

"Yes," he replied.

Why was he being so curt now? Today, at the most difficult hour of my life when we were about to watch me being lowered into the ground? I needed emotional support, and Martin was being kind of an asshole.

"But I don't want to," I said.

"Then I'll drop you off at the Institute," he said.

Heh, that's what he was planning the whole time! My body is being taken away, my morgue drawer reassigned, and he thinks in all seriousness he can just ditch me in that hideous high-rise?

"What am I supposed to do there?" I asked.

Now I had him. Martin froze in mid-motion. His fingers, which wanted to tie his shoelaces, started to tremble. Well, my dear Martin, you apparently didn't think that far in advance. My only Attachment Figure in the whole, entire world is YOU! I didn't think I'd ever be able to shake the panic I saw shooting through his brain. His best friend now thought he was overworked—at the very least. But in any case Gregor hadn't believed a single word, that was quite clear. Other people such as his colleagues and managers would certainly not be as ginger in their assessment of his mental health. Crazy, they'd say, and Martin—I could sense it at this moment with full-on clarity—was starting to firmly embrace the notion that he would in fact go crazy if I kept haunting around in his head.

"I think you should come," he said in a less-than-firm voice. "Maybe it'll be good for you to see your parents one more time."

Now I was the one who was shocked. My parents. Oh, God.

No one said anything.

Maybe that was his idea. For me to cleave back to my parents, leave him in peace, and move back home. Back into my old room with posters of Ferraris and Pamela Anderson on the wall. But my room probably didn't exist anymore; my father had presumably converted it into a study, or my mother into a dressing room. Whatever it was, I would go along to my funeral because I knew very well that otherwise I would obsess night after night about what it had been like. How my parents had looked. What my coffin looked like, and whether I would have liked the grave site. I slipped behind Martin through the living room door, climbed into the trash can with him, and was silent, just like him. You might have taken us for an old married couple the way we were driving to my funeral, each lost in our own thoughts.

The cemetery looked the way cemeteries do in winter. The tall trees, which surely cast a friendly, calming green shimmer over the graves in springtime, were now bare and thus looked like shit. I've never been one for bare trees. Whether capped with snow or not, in sun or fog: I think they just look dead.

The wide pathways through the cemetery were muddy, and there were lanterns on many of the graves with those awful candles in their little plastic cups burning inside. In the dark they always make the cemetery look haunted with all those little lights flickering everywhere.

I was familiar with this cemetery because my grandmother was buried here, and my parents used to come visit at least twice a year, on Gran's birthday and on some other sad day in November. They would light one of those little flickering lights and pretend to pray for a while before going back home and shoveling cake into their mouths. I had to go along until I was twelve, and then my father stopped going, too. I have no idea how long my mother kept up the tradition. Starting tomorrow, though, she could visit two graves at once. My birthday happens to be in November, so maybe she can cover the November visits at the same time, too. More practical.

Martin found his way to the cemetery chapel without getting lost, although as far as I was concerned the paths all looked the same. I never knew if I should take the third or fourth crosscut, but Martin knew. He was just being precise—as always.

There was a sign in front of the chapel with my name and the time of the burial on it. My name. That queasy feeling started getting stronger. Pretty soon it would be serious.

Martin swallowed, too, even though he hadn't known me at all when I was alive. And he knew that I wasn't dead now, too. Funny thing. Should you be sadder that the body is dead, or happier that the spirit is alive? But is a life like mine, where I've got only a very restricted radius of action, really any comfort? I could feel Martin struggling with these thoughts, and I couldn't help him answer his questions. Plus, I myself didn't know what the alternative was. Would "dead" mean that my spirit just ceased to exist, as well? Or would it exist somewhere else, where other spirits were flitting around? Would we be able to talk to each other, make fun of each other, tell jokes? Keep following events on earth? Make bets? With what kind of money? I'd never given any thought to things like this when I was alive, but now, in view of my special situation, they were cropping up naturally, like a cold sore after a wet kiss.

OK, that was enough. I had to create some spiritual distance. I had to think about something nice or just about the harshness of reality, instead of drowning here in religious, philosophical, or other sentimentalities. This funeral wasn't changing anything about my current situation. What the hell difference should it make if my body was lying in a refrigerated morgue drawer or inside a box underground?

Martin entered the dim light of the chapel and sat in the second-to-last row. I stayed with him for a moment, but of course I couldn't recognize the attendees just from the back like that. Stupid. So I set out, passing along the wall nice and discreetly toward the front. My parents were sitting in the front row, and behind them a couple of aunts and uncles I hadn't seen for an eternity. The women who lived on either side of my parents' house, who apparently didn't have anything better to do, or just wanted to wear their black coats out again. And my elementary school teacher. Wow! I hadn't thought about her for ages. Back in the day I had idolized her. She was the coolest teacher at school: bleach-blond, single, smoker. All the boys in my class wanted to marry her. In those days I thought she was very young and good-looking, and that was a just decade and a half ago. Now I thought she looked old and frumpy. Still blond, still a smoker, as suggested by her yellow, nicotine-stained fingers, but I couldn't tell if she was married or not. Didn't matter now anyway. She was here, in any case, and I thought that was pretty strange. Did she feel something for me in those days, too? But if so, then she must have been pretty seriously disturbed. After all, I was ten years old and had only about seven teeth in my mouth, as I mentioned before.

My mother had hardly changed in the four years since I'd seen her last. Why should she? She's been wearing her hair that way since the nineteen seventies, and this is exactly how she looked then, too. Her corpulence was still keeping the skin of her face relatively taut—that's the benefit of extra fat pads: they keep wrinkles from forming. Her legs were stuffed into thick, black pantyhose that better hid the waning juvenescence around her ankles than did the flesh-colored ones she normally wore, but hers were still the ugli-est legs I'd ever seen in my life. A disaster for a woman who never wore pants. I used to be pretty embarrassed about my mother's legs when I still needed them to lean on. My mother looked like a country-butcher's wife, and basically that's what she was, too. Her father had been a butcher, her husband was one—at least, he was until he became a wurst manufacturer who earned money by stuffing chopped offal into artificial casings and selling them to people who believed the ham sausage actually had ham in it. Have I already mentioned that for a few years I refused to eat anything but recognizably coherent meat? That is, schnitzel and steak. But that's when I was still living at home; only the best was served at our dinner table. Later on due to lack of money I transitioned back to ground meat products. Whether a burger between two pieces of cardboard passing for bun, or currywurst, it ultimately didn't matter.

Compared to his butcher's wife, my butcher father cut a finer figure, on the outside. Tanned, only ever so slightly overweight, with stylishly short hair, rimless glasses, and a fashionably tailored black jacket. People would never have thought him capable of the less-than-fashionable blows to the head he inflicted whenever his brat of a son wasn't minding.

The brief glances my father was exchanging with my elementary school teacher also explained her attendance. Pretty ballsy bringing your mistress to the funeral of your only son—but then class (ha!) was something he'd never really had. And the assertiveness to stand up to him was something my mother had never really had, either. She knew about his affairs but played along as though nothing were going on. In front of me, the neighbors, and my mother's family. To my father she kowtowed. He gave her a housekeeping allowance, he determined what was served at the dinner table, and he selected the vacation destinations. Often enough they were places teeming with willing women. Mom pretended she didn't notice anything and wrote postcards about gorgeous beaches and nice people. The only thing she had to hold onto was me, and unfortunately that was too much for me to deal with. They were both too much to deal with: her love, and his expectations.

They had both crushed me, and here and now before my coffin both of them seemed to have conveniently forgotten all that. If I had a sentimental bent I would drivel on right now about how there was more being buried at this funeral than just a body.

I'll spare you and me the description of the other guests and bulimic priest, who was leading the devotion. The clergyman was pretending he had known and liked me, but that's probably his job. Coming out of his mouth my life also sounded way more ordinary, successful, and conformist than I'd ever thought it was, but maybe the mistake was mine.

Now, you may have noticed that so far I've been talking a lot of shit about other people to dodge the actual topic. My coffin. It was grandiose. Black. Shiny black. Like a concert grand piano you might see in the symphony halls of this world. With red roses on top. The color of love. Or of a Ferrari. Or of Pamela Anderson's bikini. It looked fucking sweet.

The priest finally finished the devotion, droning, ". . . eternal rest grant unto him, O Lord . . ." Martin winced as tinny organ music pealed out of a ghetto blaster. A couple of men came forward, grabbed hold of the cart with the casket on it, rolled it out of the chapel, and all the mourners trundled along behind. My father supported my mother, who was sobbing uncontrollably. Everyone else looked awkward or bored; only the elementary school teacher had a poker face on. And Martin looked sad. Really sad. I steered clear of his gloomy thoughts.

The other cemetery visitors that day lowered their heads as the funeral procession passed by, pretending to pray for the new admit for a moment, and some of them may have even really done so—but I bet most of them were thinking thank God it wasn't me.

Since there wasn't anything exciting happening apart from this mass shuffle to my grave, my eyes wandered around some, which is when I saw her. Miriam. I thought. I wasn't totally sure of her name. But I recognized her without a doubt. She was Gugi's little sister.

Gugi got his name because he used to talk like those babies on that TV show: some weird kind of double Dutch consisting mainly of random noises. He had a serious speech impediment, but he was the best fucking automotive painter this side of Santa Fe. He could conjure up fantastic worlds, mythical beasts, or smoking-hot women onto cars and trucks. Either following a picture or freehand— however the customer wanted it. He once covered a truck with the entire crew of the starship *Enterprise.* That rocket ship left all kinds of traffic accidents in its wake from drivers craning their necks at Captain Kirk, Spock, Bones, and the rest. Yup, he painted only the original crew. And Gugi had a little sister who we of course had never paid any attention to. Little sisters are like measles, mumps, or scarlet fever. In the early stages no one notices them, and then ultimately you end up in bed with them. Miriam—or whatever her name really was—had still been in the early stages in those days. But, holy hotrod, what was she doing here now?

I had let her distract me, so I missed the end of the procession to my grave. As I looked for Martin, everyone was already standing around the hole, and the coffin was swaying on two wooden planks over it. This kind of sucks, I thought.

The priest said another couple of words, and then the strong boys walked up to the grave and lowered the coffin into the cold, dark hole. My mother was sobbing louder now; she threw a few roses onto the casket, and then my father pulled her to his side. The other mourners each took a turn stepping forward; I'm sure you've seen that before, so I don't have to describe it in epic detail here. Everyone shook hands with my parents, took a couple of steps to the side, and then they all stood there in a group. Finally Martin walked up to my parents. Martin?!

"Hey," I yelled. "What are you doing?"

Martin wouldn't be deterred.

"My condolences," he said, shaking my father's hand.

"Thank you," my father said, then took a second look at Martin. "I'm sorry; I don't think we know each other."

"No," Martin confirmed. "But I, uh, knew your son."

"Martin, cut that shit out," I said, genuinely irritated. "What are you going to tell them? That I'm living in the basement at your Institute and that I frequently piss you off?"

"Where did you know him from?" my mother asked, still sobbing.

"I, uh, he gave me a tip once in a murder case that I was investigating," Martin said.

"A murder case?" my father said. "Figures—that boy sank so low. He got mixed up with the wrong kinds of people."

"No, no," my do-gooder here hastened to reassure them. "He only passed on a piece of information. He didn't have anything to do with the crime."

Nice phrasing there, if he was talking about this case that I had taken over the lead on, because near as I can recall there wasn't another case where I'd have passed on any valuable information to him.

"So you're with the police?" my father asked.

"From the forensics unit," Martin said. I had the impression that he wasn't using this circumlocution for the first time.

"How was he doing, then?" Mom asked. "Was he OK?"

"Yes, he was doing well," Martin said, but I sensed that the question was throwing him off track a bit. In fact, he had absolutely no idea how I was doing, or rather, had been doing. He had never asked me what my life had been like. Or where I'd lived. And that made me wonder what was actually going to happen with my apartment.

"What are they going to do with my apartment?" I asked.

"His apartment looked so . . ." My mother was searching for the right words. "So depressing."

"A shithole," my father said, correcting her.

Martin was terribly embarrassed; he didn't know what he was supposed to say.

"It was a temporary solution," Martin finally said.

"On his way to homelessness," my father said. "He threw in the towel on his apprenticeship."

Yeah, well, Einstein dropped out of school, too, as I always used to retort back in the days before he threw me out of the house. "Anyone who eats at my table must finish his apprenticeship," was what he would say.

"The master mechanic is always picking on me," I would say.

"Well then he must have a reason to," my father said.

He was right, of course. The master mechanic was envious. I was the best auto freak who had ever worked in that dive. I only needed to listen to an engine to know what was wrong with it. DTC reader software, inspection checklists: kids' stuff. Me, I would turn the key and just know what was up. Plus, I could break into any car within thirty seconds. They dispatched me just three weeks into my apprenticeship when a customer lost his key. Me. Not the master mechanic. This kind of cramped his style, which I didn't know at the time, because he used to go squeeze in a lay every time he left the workshop. That's why it always took him so long when he was sent out. Because he had at least eight fillies raring to go, who were all apparently just waiting for some yuppie to accidentally toss his car keys into the trash along with his burger wrapper. And then the master mechanic would be off to help both the yuppie and some über-horny little mouse right after that.

And then I came along. I could break into cars like a world champion, and I'd be back at the workshop in less than thirty minutes. The owner liked that, but the master mechanic didn't. From then on every day meant putting up with the master mechanic's hazing.

And that's not even mentioning the meager pay. So one day after I'd pulled the emergency car-door-opening routine for, let's say, a third customer, I got even more shit unloaded on me at work, and then the stress from my mom at home was of course pissing me off, too, and I just hit my limit, ditched the apprenticeship, and moved out. That was four years ago. My mother didn't even try to get in touch with me, presumably because my father forbade her. That's how things were at our house.

Here and now I'd hit my limit again. My father made me sick, although I somehow felt sorry for my mother, even though at the same time I despised her. What kind of mother lets someone forbid her from getting in touch with her only child? I didn't want anything else to do with either of them.

"Martin, stop lying to people and start paying attention to more important things," I said.

Martin said goodbye to my parents and slowly walked toward the exit.

"Kitty corner behind you to the right is a girl," I said, and Martin turned around with a jerk.

"I think her name is Miriam, or something like that."

"Who is she?" Martin asked.

"The sister of a former buddy," I said. "I want to know what she's doing at my funeral."

"You don't mean you want me to just walk over to her and ask that?" Martin said.

"Well, yeah, dude," I replied. "There's got to be a reason, because I hardly knew her. Maybe her being here has something to do with my murder."

Martin hesitated. All of this was terribly embarrassing to him, I could sense that clearly.

"Well, get going," I pressed, and he gave in.

She was still standing a ways back from the grave, from my grave to be exact, and as we came closer we could see she had tears in her eyes. What the?

"Hello. My name is Martin Gänsewein."

She had masterful self-control and didn't start giggling or grinning or anything on mention of his silly name. She just nodded at him.

"Did you know him well?" Martin asked politely.

Miriam, who I was still hoping was named Miriam, since she didn't introduce herself, sniffled. And shook her head.

"I did," Martin said. "He told me about you."

Her flood of tears redoubled.

"You're the sister of the artist, right?"

"Artist?" She looked at him like he'd just informed her that a large, green mushroom was growing out of the top of her head. "He called Gugi an artist?"

Martin was somewhat annoyed by her completely dumbfounded expression, and I was annoyed because he had apparently taken note of my whole stream of thoughts from before, which I now found a little embarrassing.

"Yes, an artist. That's what he called him," Martin confirmed, hesitating as though he had to think back and make sure he'd noted the right information under the right name.

Miriam erupted into loud bawling.

"He always used to make fun of Gugi and I, especially of Gugi," she sobbed. "Because of his speech impediment."

Of Gugi and ME! roared Martin's internal grammar check, but he held back.

I did not! I screamed inside, but I kept my trap shut, too.

"I'm sure he was just teasing," Martin suggested, but his intonation expressed his doubt just as clearly as his face.

"Did you use to make fun of him?" he asked me sternly.

"Within the normal range," I said.

"So, that would be a yes," Martin determined. Disappointedly, I noticed. "I'm thinking that you were a pretty big asshole while you were alive, huh."

Hearing the word *asshole* within the convolutions of Martin's brain, at the edge of my open grave to boot, nearly cost me all my self-control. Only Miriam's presence saved me—and Martin.

"Just ask her why she's here," I said. Miriam beat him to it.

"I liked him, despite all that," she whispered.

"Oh," Martin said. "I'm sorry."

And that's exactly how he meant it, too, that dickface. He was sorry she had liked such an asshole. If this guy was supposed to be my only friend on earth, then I'd rather not have any more friends. None at all. That would clearly be better.

"He could also be funny," she mumbled.

"See?" I said.

"Somehow he was a loser, too, but still sweet," she said.

"I was not a loser," I roared.

"Yes," Martin said, fervently. "He really was a loser."

"Traitor," I yelled.

"But sweet," Miriam repeated.

"Do you need a ride anywhere?" Martin asked.

Now he was making his move—that is not right! I was angry, furious, enraged. I was beyond pissed off. I . . .

OK, I'll be honest: I was mad at myself. For years I'd been hauling whatever worthless skanks into bed with me, as long as they had gigantic tits and opened the gas cap when the nozzle came. Meanwhile here was a rather mousy but undoubtedly very sweet girl like Miriam who had somehow liked me, and I had no clue. And even if I had, I'd have presumably given her the brush-off with a dirty grin on my face because the dimensions of her breasts fell far short of my minimum standard. And what else mattered when it came to women?

Suddenly I made myself sick. Really. Here I was, standing at my own grave wondering how much of the shit that had happened in my life was actually my fault. Thoughts like these aren't really particularly pleasant when you're alive, but if you ask yourself these questions in time you can still change something. Become a better person, et cetera. But in my case: too late! No insight, however clever it might be, could help me now.

My brain waves were definitely headed in the wrong direction, because I didn't want to go all sentimental again, like those old ladies who rake the graves and plant those ugly, purple-colored weeds on them that look like they were the only plant that managed to survive a nuclear war. So I banished all thoughts like that from my mind and whooshed along behind Martin and Miriam, who walked back up to my grave and looked at it for a short moment, staring at the shiny black coffin, and then turned toward the exit. And that's when we saw him.

My funeral was turning into a kind of class reunion. But this particular guest was neither invited nor welcome. Miriam saw him at the same time I did, and she whispered, "Oh, shit," although such words wouldn't normally pass her lips.

Pablo. Greasy as ever, his longish black crimps glued down to his head with some kind of glistening slime, acne scars all over his face, and seven or maybe more gold hoops through his left ear. Someone in an extremely inebriated state once suggested that he get a ring through his nose, too. Twenty-four hours and a few strong blows to the back of the head later that someone woke up to find he had a ring through *his* nose. Since then no one has cracked any more jokes about the ugliest toro north of the Pyrenees.

Now here was Pablo at the cemetery. The Pablo who had, over the course of two years, sold me certain substances that were subject to trade restrictions pursuant to the Controlled Substances Act. The Pablo who was of the firm conviction that I had landed him in the pen. The Pablo who several interviewed persons had assumed was the one who had pushed me to my death.

Miriam had apparently also heard this rumor because she started laying into him like a madwoman.

"You dare show up here?" she yelled, taking long strides toward him. "Couldn't you tell from the bridge that he was dead?"

Pablo just kept leaning against the tree, pretending not to hear her.

"Who is that?" Martin asked, and I quickly filled him in. Martin was anything but enthusiastic.

Meanwhile Miriam had reached Pablo. She stood in front of him at arm's length, hands on her hips, and glared at him. God's avenging angel in sneakers!

"How perverted are you, that you would dare to show your face here at his funeral?" she asked.

"I want to be sure he's dead," Pablo calmly replied. Incidentally, he had no accent; if anything he sounded like he was from just an hour or so north of Cologne, from the Ruhr, and not from Barcelona. "I wasn't the one who bumped him off."

"Right, like I should believe you?" Miriam snarled. "Half of town thinks it was you."

"Half of town is saying it was me so no one will notice it was them," Pablo said. "In any case, I wouldn't have broken just his neck."

Martin, who had stopped a few steps back, winced. Welcome to real life, Buddy.

Miriam and Pablo continued their shouting match, and I thought Miriam held her own pretty well. Actually, I suddenly thought she was very attractive and brave and all that. She actually had me stuck in a trance for a while so I didn't notice one important fact: the setting of the scene had shifted almost without anyone noticing. Pablo was doing it very slickly, but as a dealer in illegal drugs one of course has to be pretty damned careful. In that line of work you develop an eye for dark corners that cannot be seen into from where other people are standing. He had pulled back into a dark corner like that by repeatedly taking just one small step, and then another, and Miriam and Martin had followed him like rats behind the Pied Piper. Before I could warn Martin, it happened. Pablo grabbed Miriam by the hair and pulled her with him two steps back into the bushes, and then we heard an open palm slap against a face.

"Hey," Martin yelled, taking a half step forward but stopping again and mumbling, "Shit, this can't be happening," but then he shot forward anyway. Given his frame of mind, I don't need to comment further—he had let the S-word pass his lips, after all. And in this succinct and pithy assessment of the situation he was completely correct.

Pablo had hit Miriam on the side of the head twice, making her cheeks flush red, and then she tried to land a sharp kick right in the middle of his favorite intersection. He had turned around, grabbed hold of her foot, and threw her down in one swift motion. He was kneeling on her legs when Martin arrived on the scene.

Martin apparently has never seen *Die Hard*. Or *Terminator, Triple X,* or the other summer blockbusters with more dead people in them than assistant directors. At most he's seen one *James Bond* movie, but then I bet only one with one of the older gentlemen like Sean Connery or Roger Moore. That was Martin's handicap. Because he tried talking to Pablo, when any movie aficionado with better than 20/800 vision could see the only way to move forward was with sheer force. So Martin had hardly opened his mouth when Pablo's fist slammed into his cheekbone.

It didn't shatter anything. It's not like in the movies, where the whole jaw breaks and what not. Instead, a different response is completely normal, which they always get totally wrong in the movies. The guy who receives a real swing to the cheekbone ends up toppling over in the mud.

And that's where he lies for a little while, in most cases. So, too, with Martin.

Meanwhile Miriam had dug her fingernails into Pablo's ugly mug and scratched several nice, long welts into him. As he turned back to her, she punched him in his soft parts with her right hand. You see, women can not only kick where it hurts; they can also punch. Pablo hadn't counted on that. He was still crouching on top of her legs holding her down, but after that last blow to his chicken nuggets his face turned pale as death and he slowly slumped to the side. Martin struggled back to his feet, Miriam frantically pulled her legs free, rolled over, and stood on both feet before the rest of us could really see how she'd done that. She tugged Martin by his hood out of reach of Pablo's legs, but she wasn't fast enough. The heel of Pablo's shoe somehow hit Martin's shin, he howled but didn't fall down again, instead limping along as fast as he could behind Miriam.

I had to stand by and watch the whole miserable scene with a seething rage in my gut. But I couldn't take it out on anyone. God, how I'd have loved to plant my heel into Pablo. No matter where. But, no, poor fucking impotent poltergeist that I am, I couldn't let off my steam in any way. Everyone else definitely had it better!

Only they didn't know how much they should appreciate it. At least, not Martin. He was softly groaning, holding his hand over his cheek and trying to hold his other hand over his shin, although of course that didn't work since he was running. Miriam still had hold of his duffle coat, yanking him quickly toward the exit.

"What was that?" Martin asked, not very eloquently.

"That was Pablo," Miriam said. There were tears in her eyes. "He's a first-class asshole."

"You don't say," Martin muttered as he ran his tongue around the inside of his mouth to identify any internal injuries.

"We're going to the police," Martin said after his search turned up nothing.

"No way," Miriam said. "For the moment we're even. If we go to the police, he will take out some nasty revenge on us."

"Even?" Martin asked incredulously.

"Yes, even," Miriam said. "And that's that."

———

Martin took Miriam home and then drove to the Institute for Forensic Medicine. There was a moderate uproar among his colleagues as he arrived with dirt on his jacket, ripped pants, and unmistakable swelling from being punched in the face. The boss who came running over wanted to know what had happened, and Martin somehow cooked up a wild story of mistaken identity, backed up by exclamations of dismay and occasional brow-furrowing, then he had Katrin patch him up and gave in to his boss, who sent him home. The stares of his colleagues and superiors as they followed his departure spoke volumes. In any case I had the impression that they hadn't bought his story from the get-go, particularly recalling the one or two strange, not to mention unsettling, new behavioral patterns he'd been displaying over the past few days. For example, freaking out during my autopsy, talking to "himself" in the break room, his absent-mindedness often accompanied by fervent head-shaking, his frequent visits to the morgue for no discernible reason, or just his overall nervousness and irritability, which were actually uncharacteristic of Martin. Martin, however, didn't notice the stares, and that was definitely a good thing for the moment.

A bandaged Martin drove in his bandaged trash can to the car shop, had his window replaced as he sat on one of the two chairs in the waiting room, clinging to a paper cup full of foul-smelling coffee that the nice mousy girl at the service desk had brought him. He sat that way for almost two hours, motionless like an Egyptian statue, apart from occasionally moving his left arm to put the cup to his mouth and back down again. The bruise on his cheek had started to look like a red-currant thumbprint cookie, and the thin skin under his eye was turning a similar color. He looked scary.

After the trash can was finally repaired, Martin drove home, carefully took a shower to avoid grazing his shin, and went to bed. Great!

Now here I was alone with the city maps again. But instead of learning medieval street names by heart, I considered whether I should believe Pablo or not. I couldn't really decide. I did think he was capable of murder in any case, and it presumably wouldn't have been his first. People used to gossip that he put a guy on ice for calling him a "flaming fairy." Maybe that guy had hit a nerve. But no one with a brain bigger than a piece of rabbit poop would be stupid enough to try and find out the truth.

I wasn't getting anywhere this way; all this brooding wasn't helping, plus it's not my kind of thing. If I still had a body, on a day like this I'd have crashed in front of the boob tube downing one beer after the other, and at some point I'd have blissfully passed out into a coma. However, if at the time—that is, during my life—I had known how little time I had left on earth, I would've enjoyed this near-daily pastime perhaps a bit less often. Now, by contrast, I had until the end of time, but no access to either boob tube or beer.

I was just wondering if I should wake Martin up to turn the idiot box on when the phone rang. Surprised, I realized that it had gotten dark out, and the clock showed seven thirty already. Martin was still napping. The phone kept ringing. After the twelfth ring it stopped, but then immediately started again. Martin appeared at the bedroom door, groped for the phone, and whispered, "Yes?"

"Martin?" a voice asked, which after a moment's thought we both recognized as Birgit's.

"Yes?" Martin whispered again. "What time is it?"

Birgit burst out crying. "My car's gone," she said, hard to understand through her sobs.

"What do you mean 'gone'?" Martin asked.

"Stolen," Birgit said, sniffling then crying louder.

"Did you already report it to the police?" Martin asked.

"Yeahahaha," she sobbed. "But they said there wasn't much hope . . ."

"Now, don't be so upset," Martin said in a voice so velvety soft you could still hear the cozy comforter he'd just emerged from. "You can buy yourself . . ."

"Ooh hoo hoo," pierced out of the receiver. ". . . any money . . . not insured yet . . . never have something like that again," was all we could make out.

"The car wasn't insured?" Martin asked. "Nooo! "

Martin literally melted in compassion for that chick who'd bought herself a hot ride and then was too stupid to insure the thing. The man had a big heart, I thought. The first thing I'd have done is chew her out. Not Martin.

He said, "Oh, Birgit. Please don't be so upset. Maybe they'll find it, your car. It's pretty conspicuous."

"But," sniffle, sniffle, "the police said that it was definitely an organized ring that steals classic cars like that on order, and then the car is out of the country the same night."

The moment she said "organized ring," a jolt went through Martin. His neurons were all a-tingle. He straightened up in his fleecy terrycloth pajamas, stretched, and said, "Actually, maybe there's a way for someone to do something."

A banner was unfurling in his brain, as big as one of those sheets that soccer fans hold up in the stadium for their favorite players. But Martin's banner read: "Now you can do something for me!"

And by "you" he meant me.

And a certain other name popped into Martin's thoughts, decorated with a hundred exclamation points: Olli!

You remember: Olli's the guy I stole the SLR for that I found the body in . . . well, you know the story.

Of course there wasn't any guarantee that Olli had anything to do with Birgit's stolen Beemer, but the chances were a hundred to one.

I wasn't listening to Martin's quiet muttering into the phone anymore at all, and instead I was wondering how best to proceed.

"Tell her we need the license number, the VIN, and the car key," I quickly told Martin before he could hang up. Birgit promised to get everything together.

"Then let's get going."

Martin looked horrible. He had bags even under his nondiscolored eye, making it look as though his tears of late were made of squid ink; the coloration of the bruise had reached its maximum luminosity; and his eyes—well, they were something. His look had changed. In place of the friendly, sincere, and innocent way he used to look at the people around him, in the past few days a kind of irritated fatigue had taken over instead. Or a tired testiness, seasoned with a pinch of fuck-off. Especially now as he was mumbling with Birgit in that cuddly voice, you could make out mainly only the fatigue, but when he turned to speak to me the whole load of negativity burst through his pupils. Great, now I was the Bad Guy again, and I hadn't even beaten him up. Plus, I was even prepared to help him with his girlfriend's car. A little gratitude would have been very much in order. Or some kind of deal. That'd be even better. He'd have to promise me . . .

Martin came back out of the bedroom dressed, his hair nicely parted, and he looked like Mommy's Favorite again. Just still wearing that little wool coat. . . I contemplated whether Olli would take him seriously if he saw him like this. On the other hand, Olli and anyone else who ran into this guy would immediately know he's not dangerous. That's good when you're placing yourself directly into the lion's den. So I didn't say anything. Not about his clothes, anyways.

"Martin," I started with my deal. "I'm prepared to help you recover Birgit's car."

Martin didn't hesitate once. "Great," he said.

"I'll do it if you promise me you'll keep investigating my murder case."

Now he started playing the pillar of salt.

"So, what do you say?" I whined, getting sick of the stupid way he was acting. He reminded me of those guys who paint their faces white, throw on a bed sheet, and stand out on some street corner—and then want people to give them money for not moving. I'd always thought that was crazy.

"I might have thought that after everything I've already done for you it would go without saying that you would help me now," he said.

"And tomorrow you'll piss off and leave me sitting in this shit all alone," I said, and I could sense that the idea had already occurred to him.

"No," he said, reluctantly. "I will keep helping you. But right now Birgit's car is at the top of our list."

Martin is a man of honor, which is why I was satisfied with this promise. We left the apartment, scraped the ice off the windows of his trash can, picked up the car keys from Birgit, whom we did not bring along—for her own safety—and drove to Olli's.

Olli's got a used-car lot out on the arterial. It looks just the way you'd imagine, including little pennants and giant signs with the prices on them, trying to give the impression the cars are a good value. Naturally they aren't. Prices like that never are, which actually goes without saying.

Olli was there of course, sitting with his legs apart on his desk chair staring at Martin as he entered the office. Olli's always there, even though he doesn't live there. No one knows where Olli lives; maybe he doesn't know himself anymore, which is why he's always at his car lot. It happens only very rarely that he's not there, and then it's only for a couple of hours. People say.

I started with a quick spin around to get oriented, and this was really the first time that I felt like my immateriality was pretty frigging cool. I floated over the lot, staring into every corner, and then—and this would have been totally impossible for a flesh-and-blood person—I snuck into the big shop that was toward the back of the property.

In the front part was the workshop and the paint booth, the finest equipment anywhere and with an excellent reputation beyond the city limits. Regular customers could come in this far, too. But the shop extended even farther behind the paint booth, which you couldn't really tell either from the outside or the inside. You had to know it, and I knew it. And there, between the fat BMWs, Daimlers, Jags, and even a couple of Audis, was Birgit's baby. Some dark-haired, dark-skinned men were standing among the cars, talking in a language unknown to me. I didn't pay much attention to them, but I thought I'd seen one or another of them before at some point. Especially the tall guy. But that didn't matter now. I tore back to

Martin, reported my discovery, and made my way toward the office with him.

Martin and I had discussed our action plan, which is why right now I had nothing to do other than observe.

"Are you Olli?" Martin said in greeting. He kept his hands in his pockets.

Martin and I had haggled for ten minutes on this point of the plan alone. I'd explained to him that he had to be cool. He had to immediately make clear that he knows not only the name on the office door but also the nicknames, especially Olli's, and he certainly shouldn't try to be genteel. So, no hand-shaking. By acting this way Olli would immediately know that Martin wasn't just another normal prospective used-car buyer.

Martin by contrast didn't want to be either impolite or provocative. He rubbed his colorful cheek and declared that he really didn't feel at all like provoking anyone. Understandable, but bullshit. For our plan to work he had to exude cool self-confidence. Yes, Martin! You can see we're treading on pretty fucking thin ice. But what all wouldn't a man do to get his sweetheart to stop bawling?

"What can I do for you?" Olli asked back.

I'd noticed the vigilance-switch flip on in Olli's eyes, which almost disappeared between his fat cheeks and fat eyelids.

"I'm looking for a car," Martin said.

"Settled on something?" Olli asked. Complete sentences weren't really his thing.

"Settled," Martin said. "A BMW 3-Series convertible from the early 1980s, tiptop condition, grey exterior, red leather interior."

Olli sort of jiggled a couple of times, which could mean he was laughing or that he might be exploding in the near future.

"Hard to get," Olli said.

"No," Martin said. "Hard to keep."

We'd practiced this script over and over, because if Olli can spare brainpower and words, he'll save both—which is why his standard phrases are predictable. However, one should not assume he has no brainpower. Olli is clever, which is why he's the fattest fish in the pond of hot-car dealers. He knew that Martin knew that that convertible had been stolen. We even knew that it was in back in his shop. But Olli didn't yet know that we knew, and we couldn't hurl disses at him, either, since that'd be a provocation. But with Olli you didn't need to lay everything out straight, either; with him you just had to strike the right chord, and I knew that chord. I hadn't worked for Olli for years for nothing. I knew Olli as well as a small-time car thief with golden hands can know his client.

We'd find out right away if that was good enough.

Olli didn't say anything and stared at Martin; Martin didn't say anything and stared at Olli.

"How much do you want to spend?" Olli asked. Also standard.

"I propose a wager," Martin said, without real conviction.

Olli jiggled again; I hoped he was laughing. "A wager? Well, let's hear it," he said.

Martin swallowed. "My girlfriend Birgit used to have a car like that," he started in a trembling voice. "She saved up a couple of years until she could afford it. She's totally crazy about cars, and at some point it just had to be that one."

Olli's eyes disappeared almost completely behind his rolls of fat, which were squeezing out from top to bottom.

"After a couple of days the car disappeared," Martin continued. We had agreed that the verb "to steal" in all its principal parts would be avoided entirely.

"She was howling her eyes out, for two specific reasons: first, she loved that car, and second, it wasn't insured yet."

Olli bent forward, to the extent that this was at all possible with his galactic corpulence. "Not insured?" he asked. A small twinkle appeared in his left eye. We were on the right track!

Martin shook his head.

"And what's your deal?" Olli asked.

Martin shrugged. "I don't care about cars, but I love my girlfriend."

Now! It had to be about to happen, I thought, and, bingo! We'd done it. Olli was crying. Thick tears were running down his cheeks; he was sincerely touched that this wool-wearing gnome had the courage to enter this lion's den and get his sweetheart's car back. The fattest guy since Jabba the Jigglemonster from *Star Wars* just so happens, when he has time, to spend the entire day watching the sappiest romance movies conceivable. His personal DVD collection ranges from silent black-and-white films to animated movies and everything in between that the lachrymal-gland-squeezers in Hollywood, Bollywood, and wherever else in the world had ever captured on celluloid. And he watches all of them again and again. And he weeps during every movie, even when watching it for the twentieth time. *And* he loves women with a weakness for cars.

Olli ranks among those men who are not embarrassed of their tears. But he doesn't make a big deal about it. He pulled a gigantic handkerchief out of his pants pocket, blew snot into it, and returned to the topic.

"You wanted to propose a wager?"

"If my girlfriend's car key fits in a car that you've got here, then I'll take that car with me."

Martin's hands were dripping with sweat, his knees were shaking, but his voice was coming across fairly sensibly. Good thing, too.

"Just like that?" Olli asked.

"Just like that," Martin confirmed.

Olli pressed a button on his phone, and in the next moment Greenbeard came in. That's not his real name of course, but one time he ate five liters of woodruff-flavored gelatin on a bet, won the pot, and five minutes later puked everything back out. In so doing, there was certain residue left in his beard. What his real name is, I've forgotten.

Olli held out his fleshy hand, and after a brief hesitation Martin put the key into it. Olli handed the key to Greenbeard, and whispered a few sentences into his ear. There wasn't anything we could do but wait.

That was the most dangerous moment of this whole operation. Olli might bag the key and demand a surcharge from his end customer for that, but my senses told me he would stick to the deal. And in fact after three rather long minutes, the BMW drove out, pulling up to the entrance.

"Come on, we're getting out of here," I told Martin, who was standing in front of Olli's desk the whole time sweating blood and water.

"Just a moment," Olli said as Martin turned around. "How did you know that you would bust the bank here with your wager?"

Martin shrugged. "It was a message from Sam," he said with a wink. "Thanks," he added afterward, but he got no answer because Olli was already weeping again.

We stepped over to the car, climbed in, and drove to Birgit's place.

Birgit was overjoyed. She drove Martin back to Olli's, where the trash can was still parked on a side street, Martin got into the trash can and Birgit into the BMW, and everyone went home, happy and content. Except for me, once again no one was paying attention to me; I was bored, and Martin had forgotten to turn on the TV again.

SIX

Martin's boss was nice about Martin getting to work a half hour late. He took Martin aside and asked him in a collegial tone if he was feeling fit enough to work again, and all that claptrap. I listened in a bit and then went in search of Katrin. She was already deep in conversation with Jochen.

". . . acting pretty strange, the past few days," I heard her say. "And then this mugging on top of it all. But he won't say anything. I'm slowly starting to get worried."

Ah ha, they were talking about Martin. His colleagues were gossiping already.

Meanwhile the guy they were gossiping about was pleased as Punch, because visiting him at his desk was none other than Birgit.

". . . as just a little thank-you. Because you were having such a hard time with the old headset and its cord was bugging you."

Scattered on Martin's desk was enough packaging for Christmas and birthday combined, and his right ear was covered by an earpiece that concealed almost his entire outer ear, with a little boom sticking out in front that presumably contained the mic. Boy, he totally looked like crap in it, though, with his shiner on the left and this cyborg ear on the right, but Birgit was beaming at him. What exactly was this woman's ideal of male beauty? She probably voted for

Alf as Sexiest Man Alive and went soft at the knees seeing the party leaders on the floor of the Bundestag.

Martin in any case was smiling in bliss, dictating "Birgit is the greatest" into his computer. Cool, huh? I left the two love birds to their cooing and roamed through the building in search of something more exciting. Gregor struck me as not the worst option. He was standing in the lobby with his cell phone to his ear, fumbling in his chest pocket for a pen.

"Yeah, go ahead," he mumbled once he'd found it. He sank down onto one of the chairs in the lobby, took a pad of paper out of his jacket's side pocket, and jotted down some address that didn't ring a bell for me right off the bat. Except that it was in the area where Martin and I had gotten our heads smashed in the night before last looking for information about the dead woman.

"And the witness, what's her name?" Gregor asked, listening carefully and writing a name down. Ekaterina Szszcyksmcnk. All right, obviously that wasn't really her name, but I found her last name impossible to remember; it was just a string of random consonants no normal person could possibly pronounce.

"And she was certain she recognized the woman from the pictures in the paper?" Gregor asked. I couldn't hear the answer.

"Does she know her name?"

Brief pause.

"Too bad. Oh well. Still, it's a starting point at least. I'll head over there now."

He hung up, said hi to Birgit, who was apparently on her way out, as he walked past her to take the elevator to Martin's floor. Martin was sitting at his computer, dictating words that aroused him, such as "multiple perforations of the lung" and "a strikingly well-defined margin resulting from the use of a dull tool causing separation at the root of the penis." I turned my attention to other things. More beautiful things. Katrin, who was watering the ferns. I fawned around her a bit, but of course she didn't notice me. Really too bad. It could've been so nice going out on a double date. Martin and Birgit, me and Katrin.

Martin had stopped describing what were apparently the fatal results of some real-life telenovela, so I turned my attention to him and Gregor to get my hands, as it were, on the latest information. But first Gregor subjected his friend to a highly embarrassing interrogation.

"What the hell happened to you?" was the opening line.

"It's not that bad," Martin said, heroically.

Poser. Yesterday he was crying his eyes out, and now today he was pretending he was an American soldier whose kneecaps can get shot to smithereens without a wince or whimper.

"Yeah, I can tell . . ." Gregor said. "Geez, your head slips off your pillow and hits the mattress, and this is how you come to work!"

Martin smiled ruefully. "I guess we've known for some time that hard mattresses are definitely not as healthy as people used to assume. Maybe I should buy myself a new one."

Birgit's visit seemed to have cheered him up dramatically; now he was even making little jokes at his own expense.

Gregor didn't smile. "I hope you filed a report with the police."

Martin shook his head. "Against the mattress?"

He was going to carry this number mercilessly through to the curtain; I wouldn't have thought him capable of that.

"We've got some leads on that anonymous woman," Gregor said. "I'm telling you this so you'll stop sniffing around on your own and getting yourself all clobbered up."

"Who is she?" Martin asked.

Gregor shook his head.

"Does your information match my, uh, research?" Martin added.

"No comment."

"Man, Gregor. We've talked about cases before; we're a good team," Martin said.

He looked disappointed or sad; I couldn't interpret his hangdog look exactly.

"Yes, we're a good team, as long as you stick to your autopsy tools and your brain—and stop using your fists."

Martin didn't say anything.

"I only want to protect you," Gregor said. "First off, so you quit taking a couple blows to the jaw every day, and, second, so you avoid stress on the job. I mean real stress. You do know that the district attorney will kick you in your coroner's ass if you interfere with official police business by conducting your own investigation and withholding information. You're still part of the criminal prosecution, after all. You could lose your job."

That hit the mark. Martin grew pale as a ghost.

"In addition, you seem to have a penchant for picking fights with people who don't wear kid gloves. If what you've told me is true, then there have already been two murders in this case, and they're somehow connected. Do you think people like that will balk at murdering some piddly little coroner?"

Martin slumped in his chair.

Gregor laid his hand on Martin's shoulder. "Think about what I've said, and go to the movies, or ask Birgit out to dinner, or some other innocuous activity to get your mind off things."

Martin nodded weakly, and Gregor gave him another friendly pat on the shoulder before leaving.

"Well that's some news!" I said.

Martin winced. "Were you listening in?"

"Of course," I said, in a good mood.

"Then you understand that Gregor didn't actually cough up the information we need. I can't do anything more."

Ha, he can't seriously believe he can get out of this whole business that easily, can he?

"The witness who recognized the photo in the paper of your lovely body is named Ekaterina Something and lives only a couple of steps away from the club where we talked to that bouncer," I said. No—I cheered.

"How do you know that?" Martin asked, devoid of enthusiasm.

I told him about the advance information I had. He hesitated.

"The witness is totally harmless; she won't do anything to us. We'll just go over there and ask her about everything she knows about the dead woman," I said.

"How do you know that she's harmless?" Martin asked with clearly discernible doubt.

"Because she reported it to the police herself," I said. God, you had to explain everything to him.

"I'll give her a call," Martin said.

"Good idea," I said. "Look her up in the phone book under Ekaterina Something."

Martin didn't say anything.

"Tonight we'll drive past her place on the way home," I decided. *Basta.*

Martin went back to his work and turned on the mic, which he sets to PAUSE when he's not currently dictating anything. He had not agreed, but he hadn't shot me down, either. So in high spirits I repeated the word that Italians use to close a discussion: *basta.*

On Martin's screen the word *basta* appeared. We both stared at it for a few seconds. Speechless.

"Where did that come from?" Martin asked aloud.

"From me," I answered.

Both of those sentences appeared on screen, as well.

We stared again.

"Say something else," Martin thought.

Nothing happened on the screen.

"How does the headset connect to the computer?" I asked.

That question was written out, too.

"Infrared port? Or Bluetooth? Or is that the same thing?" Martin thought, but he didn't speak it aloud. No reaction.

"Cool," I thought, and that word appeared in neat black letters.

"I like this kind of connection," I said. "That's exactly what I was looking for with the TVs, so I can turn them on myself when they're on standby."

Again the sentence was written, but instead of *standby* the words *sand fly* appeared on the screen.

"Hey," I yelled. "What happened there?"

"Unless you pronounce things very clearly, the program will misunderstand a word now and again," Martin explained.

"That may happen with you, but I don't mumble when I'm thinking," I said.

Martin didn't answer. He was still shocked. But then hope suddenly starting blossoming within him.

"Now there's a way for you to make yourself noticeable," he said. "You can prove to Gregor and the others that you exist."

I had to think about that for a moment. Big time. I said as much to Martin, who couldn't understand my hesitation at all. I didn't feel like discussing it with him now, and I receded into my thoughts.

Should I have been happy? Presumably. But at the moment I was confused. This new communication option was a little bit like online chat. Online chat is so fucked up you can't even imagine. People who don't even know each other meet in a chat room on the Internet and tell each other the most intimate details of their lives. Their most secret desires, their violent fantasies, their sexual preferences. Suicidal thoughts, proposals of marriage, insults: everything is blown out into the world for anyone to read. How much sicker can human beings get, actually? And how much further from reality? They fucking feel like they they're among friends in their cozy little chat rooms—but in reality they know only the ridiculous nicknames of the psychos otherwise floating around in there with them. It could be your neighbor outing himself as a serial murderer, or your own mother offering to blow you off. There is nothing human about any of it. You can't form an image of the person behind the name; all you see are letters and numbers, and you react with compassion, anger, or horror. And I should become one of them? Some invisible ghost communicating via computer screen? I imagined complimenting Katrin and then the sentence "you've got awesome tits" appearing. Or better yet, appearing with a small error: "you've got awesome nits." Would you be into that? That's what I'm saying. So for now I decided to stay clear of Martin's computer whenever he had his new headset switched on. I felt shitty enough without a body; I didn't need to end up with my voice and feelings slaughtered in some jumble of letters, too.

At some point around noon Martin did a short walkthrough of the building to check on me, and I thought that was exceptionally nice of him. That's how it should be. He still remembered I had once had a body, and he perceived me as a feeling, whole being—OK, well not entirely whole, but still, as whole as somehow possible. His concern touched me, and I could tell him that directly without having to think some carefully formulated sentence into a port. It did occur me that he might be checking on me only to keep me from getting up to no good with my newly discovered gift of communication, but I quickly pushed that thought aside. I needed a bit of support, and I was determined to find it in Martin's behavior. *Basta.*

At quitting time, Martin stopped briefly at a street food stand to pick up a veggie burger with a tofu patty and colorful side salad. That's the kind of dinner guinea pigs eat, or people with colostomy bags, but he shoveled that health fodder into his mouth with a full appetite. Meanwhile I was dreaming of a big, thick hamburger with meat, sauce, and onions gushing out on all sides, gunk running down your sleeve to your elbow. People's tastes are so different.

You could say that about Ekaterina Something as well, because her apartment, which apparently had not been updated since the war, stank of rancid grease and cabbage. Every surface that Martin touched with his hand—before he wised up—was sticky. The woman herself looked the way you would expect someone who lives in an apartment like this to look: just as greasy and sticky as everything else in her environment. Perfect camouflage, one might well say, if this woman were a chameleon and not an approximately one-hundred-year-old Russian, Belorussian, or Ukrainian—if there's any difference among those.

The idea that she'd discovered the photo of the body during her morning perusal of the *Cologne Advertiser* over coffee and rolls and then called the police is something neither Martin nor I could really picture. However, we didn't need to ask how she came across the photo, because when she opened her refrigerator door to grab some butter to set out with the dust-dry crackers for us on the table, we saw that issue of the newspaper: apparently some fishmonger had used it to wrap up the woman's purchases. The photo of the deceased girl's lovely face was wrapped around six plump sardines whose heads were bloody and eyes cloudy. The stench took Martin's breath away.

"You told the police that you recognized the woman from the photo in the paper," Martin started.

"*Da, da,* I tolt police everything."

The accent she spoke with was bad enough, but the fact that she had only a few teeth in her mouth all sticking out crooked from her lower jaw didn't improve things. I didn't want to try to imagine what Martin's computer might write if she were dictating to it.

"It would be great if you could repeat it for me," Martin said.

"Girl lived here, above me," she said.

"Do you know her name?"

She shook her head. "No name on door, never tolt me."

"Did you ever speak with her then?" Martin asked.

She nodded. "Hello and such."

"Did she speak German?"

"Yes, but mother tonkue from Balkan or such."

"Did she live alone?"

"*Da, da,* alone. But man sometimes was there."

The toothless grandma winked at Martin! I roared with laughter, but Martin winced so big that you see it even through his duffle coat.

"What kind of man?" Martin asked after pausing to recover, during which he attempted, and totally failed at, a friendly smile.

"Tall." She held up her arms in a gesture that meant more "fat" than "tall."

"Bik man with nice car," she added.

Our ears pricked up. "A small, silver, fast car?" I suggested, like the SLR, and Martin repeated the question for the grandma.

"Not small. Bik man, bik car."

Ah ha, too bad. But actually that made sense. Fat men drive fat cars.

"Did she spend a lot of time at home, or did she have a job?" Martin asked.

"In day at home, in night away."

"Maybe she served tables at a restaurant?" Martin suggested.

The grandma energetically shook her head, and then made a gesture that is understood internationally. Martin turned beet-red. The grandma grinned again and set her hand on his arm. Martin stared.

She let go of his arm. "Not on street." For the next gesture, she rubbed her thumb and index finger together.

Ah ha. She meant that the dead woman hadn't been some cheap streetwalker. But could a centenarian like this tell that? A woman who was running a shelf-life experiment in her fridge with sardines marinated in newsprint?

I answered the question for myself with a resounding yes. The woman was not stupid; she just had a strange view of modern residential environments, hygiene, and food preparation. But she had life experience, and that's what we needed here. I took her at her word.

The only thing that was still bugging me now was the question of why this woman, who so obviously lived in her own world, had contacted the police. It certainly may be a prejudice on my part, but I have never before had the impression that those of our fellow countrymen and women with a westward-oriented immigration background had any particular fondness for German law enforcement. You get what I mean, right? That Russians piss on German cops wherever and whenever they can. Martin evidently had the same idea, but articulated it in a higher linguistic register.

"Ask her," I said.

"She might interpret that as an insult," he said.

"So what?" I said. "That's actually what we want to know."

Martin asked. Worded nicely. So nicely that at first Ekaterina didn't at all understand what Martin wanted from her. Then the penny dropped.

"Where I am comink from, you can buy police like woman. Here, police goot."

Sometimes it's as simple as that. Now, in my short life I used to screw the cops over whenever I could, and here this antique matron loved the German police for their white vests, and so she performed her civic duty with great attentiveness. I was embarrassed. Secretly, of course, so Martin wouldn't notice.

We left the apartment, the building, and that neighborhood, and I asked Martin what we wanted to do with the rest of our evening now.

"I'm dropping you off at the Institute," he said. "Then I've got something else planned."

Birgit! I could feel it, even though he was exerting his maximum effort to withhold these thoughts from me. "OK," I said.

We drove to the Institute, Martin came in with me, turned the TV on in Conference Room Two, went down to the autopsy section, scrubbed his hands with hot water and disinfectant, and then called "see you tomorrow" and disappeared.

Of course I did not stay at the Institute. Late-night programming isn't so great that I want to hang out in front of it all night if I've got an alternative. And this alternative was very interesting indeed.

Previously I hadn't had much opportunity to study Birgit and Martin's relationship very closely. The relationship did seem to be pretty new, generally. So quite a bit could still happen. I kept my thoughts strictly to myself so Martin wouldn't notice I was there, and I drove with him to Birgit's place.

She had obviously been waiting for him.

When she opened the door, her blond hair was illuminated by the lamp in her foyer, giving her an authentic halo, like in those little pictures of saints from religion class at school.

The rest was not saint-suitable. Her pinstriped pants, which I was already familiar with, were pretty frigging tight, and the white sweater she was wearing today fit her grille like such a soft coat of fur that you immediately wanted to pet it. It's the same compulsion that overcomes every kid at the petting zoo. "A bunny rabbit, Mommy, a bunny rabbit!" and, presto, sticky kids' hands are running over the furry curves. Martin's hands restrained themselves effortlessly, however. I didn't trust myself to peek into Martin's brain because he wasn't supposed to notice that the evening was going to be a threesome.

"Are you hungry?" Birgit asked. "I can make you something to eat."

"No, thanks," Martin muttered. "I grabbed something on the way over at Wedschi-Päradeis."

Wait a second, I thought. Did I miss something? I ran back through the events of the evening, and then I realized: "Veggie Paradise" must have been the name of that street food stand where you can get anything except for a proper bite to eat. Namely, something made of meat. Burgers, currywurst, schnitzel, half a roasted chicken with fries: that's a proper German snack. But at the stand where Martin went there were only veggies. That has nothing to do with paradise. It should be called Herbaceous Hell. Or Parsnip Purgatory. But Birgit nodded and lead the way into the living room.

First the most important thing: there were no city maps hanging on the walls here. Also no kitschy pictures of horses with long eyelashes and wavy manes, no backlit skyline pictures, and no clowns. Hanging on the walls of Birgit's living room were vacation photos. Hundreds of them. Some with Birgit, some not. Some of big cities—I recognized Paris right away—some of landscapes that looked mainly green. Maybe Ireland? No idea.

Martin had apparently not been here yet because he went over to the walls and studied the photos while Birgit opened a bottle of white wine, filled two glasses, and brought them over to Martin.

"Cheers," she said, beaming at him.

"¡Salud!" Martin said, beaming back at her. Beaming through his eyes and his purple cheekbone.

They drank the way people drink wine. Sip by sip. Not like with beer, chugging the first can and yanking the second one open while you release the excess pressure produced in your system from the first. Nope, quite civilized here. When they set down the glasses, a disinterested observer might not have recognized that something was missing.

Martin had her explain the vacation pictures to him; it was Paris, and it was Ireland, and each picture had a little story to it. They laughed, sipped a bit of wine now and again, and the cautious touches grew more frequent. Sometimes they'd both point to the same picture and their hands would touch—gasp! Sometimes Martin would step ahead to the next picture while Birgit stayed put—body check, whoopsie!

I started missing my TV shows. Did he want to lay this piece of skirt or not? I had not come all the way over here to watch the G version of *La boum*! And apparently I had an ally in this, because right as I was about to lose my patience for real, Birgit leaned forward and kissed Martin. On the lips. Finally! I wanted to pat the bunny on her soft shoulder, but unfortunately I lacked anything to pat with.

Still, it was a start, I thought. Now surely Martin will get down to business, slide his hands under her sweater, knead her warm skin, especially over the curvy bits—and by that I don't mean her shoulders. But on this point I'd expected too much of Martin. He didn't exactly stay totally passive; he even kept holding Birgit in his arms after they finished kissing, but he didn't go any further than that. In any case, not at a speed that one might perceive with the naked eye. Apparently people who drive trash cans don't screw like people who drive Ferraris.

Subsequent overtures proceeded in slow motion. It took another seventeen minutes for the sweater to land on the couch, and another twenty-five for Birgit's pants to land next to it. Then they went into the bedroom where Martin also took off his sweater vest, shirt, pants, and socks. And off they went under the covers. At least they left the little nightlight on; I was quite grateful for that. They made out some more, felt each other up some more, all very carefully of course—but, still, we were heading in the right direction. Even Martin was getting revved up; at least he didn't have some kind of physical problem. I'll admit that was something I had been afraid of, because no normal person makes out for two hours if he doesn't have to. And you have to if you can't, you know, proceed. It's as simple as that. Martin seemed able and willing, though, but something also seemed to be holding him back. I took a chance and got closer to his thoughts, but I couldn't fathom what I found in there. Martin was hesitating because he didn't have a raincoat with him and couldn't decide if he should ask Birgit if she had one or if he shouldn't say anything at all and just keep going as though this question were totally irrelevant.

I couldn't take it anymore. I said, "Martin, stop making a big deal about it, just nail her, will you!"

His reaction was a disaster. Martin winced, everything in him went flabby, and his head writhed in a chaotic mess of ideas and feelings—horniness, shock, hatred (presumably for me), shame all mixed together. He leaped out of bed, stammered some incoherent babble in which the only understandable word was "sorry"; everything else was complete gibberish. He grabbed up all of his clothes, got dressed, apologized to Birgit once more, who was sitting in the bed bewildered, presumably wondering if she'd done something wrong or if the guy was just totally cuckoo, and he left the apartment.

I stayed with Birgit to try and console her, which of course didn't work since she couldn't hear me. She stood up, straightened up the apartment, looked unhappy, started to cry, drank another glass of white wine, although this time quite a bit faster. Funny how everything seemed to move faster when Martin wasn't here. She went back to bed but got up after a half hour and turned on the TV. After she fell asleep on the couch around one thirty I snuck out.

SEVEN

It was a calm, dark night as I floated through the streets of Cologne unsure whether I should go to Martin's place or back to the Institute. I didn't do either; instead I spirited away the rest of the night, whooshing through the city, eavesdropping on people, and trying to establish contact with them. No use. No one could perceive me, no one could hear me, no one could share their thoughts with me. I felt alone. And I felt guilty. I regretted my outburst that had ended Martin's nice evening so unpleasantly, maybe even putting an end to his relationship with Birgit, which had just been starting to blossom. I was going to have to ask him to forgive me. That's not normally my thing, but I would definitely have to make an exception in this case.

The next morning Martin and I arrived at the Institute at the same time; he was climbing out of his trash can, and just as he closed the car door I said, "Martin, I'm sorry about last night. Please forgive me."

He pretended he didn't notice me at all. For a moment I panicked, thinking that now even this last connection to the world of the living had been severed, but then I sensed the amount of effort he was devoting to not noticing me.

I waited for another moment, but he didn't give in. So I said again, "Martin, I asked you to forgive me."

No reaction.

"I'm sorry, now don't hold a grudge," I tried again.

Nothing.

Martin entered the building, went into his office, hung his duffle coat up on the coat rack, put on his lab coat, and went downstairs. There was an autopsy waiting. I stayed close to him, although I didn't look at the gory details, and I kept sending apologies in his direction. He by contrast had totally walled himself off. I begged again and again, and he ignored me again and again, in a huff. He was slowly starting to piss me off.

I gave him another hour, apologizing another three times. Then I changed tack.

He was standing alone in the break room waiting for the water for his tea to boil when I planted the idea in his brain that his fly was open. He looked down reflexively and checked the zipper—and right at the moment Katrin stepped into the break room, too. I had seen her coming; my timing was perfect. Martin blushed.

"Hello, Katrin," he mumbled.

"Hi, Martin." An embarrassed gesture toward the coffee machine. "Any coffee left?"

"Uh, yes, I think so."

Katrin squeezed past Martin, grabbed a cup from the cabinet and poured herself some coffee. "Everything OK with you?" she asked as though in passing, but her into-nation wasn't as relaxed as the question was supposed to sound.

"Yes, yes, everything's great," Martin said, the whole left half of his face purple from his bruise and his eyes blood-shot. "Everything's dandy."

"Good," Katrin said, pouring milk into her coffee and leaving the break room.

"That happened because you're ignoring me," I said. "Accept my apology and let's be friends again."

Martin didn't respond. I was starting to get really mad. What else could I do? I couldn't kneel in front of him, I couldn't hang banners from an overpass over the autobahn, I couldn't buy him a beer, and I couldn't apologize to Birgit for him.

I had been practicing the only thing I could do, for hours. I had apologized. Mountains of apologies. And still he insisted on being pigheaded. He apparently wanted no peace.

Fine. Then war it was.

———•———

Martin walked down the stairwell with a couple of his colleagues, and I screamed, "Watch out, a step is missing!" He hesitated in the middle of stairs, gripping the arm of the colleague next to him in terror and throwing him off balance. They both staggered but didn't fall. Everybody stared at Martin.

"Uh, somehow I twisted my ankle," Martin mumbled.

His colleagues gave him compassionate or concerned looks, and much too quickly they added that people did sometimes twist their ankles on these stairs, even though that was only semibelievable.

He was in the middle of an autopsy, where he was wielding the knife, and as he reached for the liver I yelled, "Don't touch!" Again he winced, his hands trembling, and his colleague with the Dictaphone staring at him with a furrowed brow. He opened the chest cavity, removed the heart, and in my saddest voice, which I normally reserve for very, very sad situations, I said, "You're hurting him."

Martin dropped the heart. He was breathing shallowly, and there were beads of sweat on his forehead. He stabbed the scalpel into the body's upper thigh and left it there jutting out, quivering. The Dictaphone guy and the dissection guy both gawked at Martin, stunned. Martin tore the mask off his face; he was as white as the wall, and his eyes were glowing frantically. He staggered to the men's room and revisited his breakfast.

"Let's be friends again," I said as he was rinsing out his mouth.

He ignored me.

His boss was waiting outside the bathroom door.

"Jochen took over the autopsy," his boss said, taking Martin by the arm. "Come on. We're going to have some tea, and you're going to tell me what's got you so frazzled."

Martin nodded. I was tense.

Of course Martin didn't say what had him so frazzled. He sipped the fancy-schmancy upland Darjeeling FTGFOP 1-2-3 garden tea that his boss orders through a licensed importer—in special packaging at a special price—and listened to his boss's spiel about the especially fine bud tips of this particular tea's leaves, the weather in the Himalayas, and the training of the women who harvest the tea leaves, but he was only half paying attention. He wasn't able to concentrate, and his boss noticed that.

"So, what's up with you then? We've known each other for twelve years, and I've never seen you like this before."

Martin looked into his teacup. "I think I'm coming down with a cold," he mumbled.

"That may be," replied his boss, who of course was also a doctor. Specifically a corpse doctor, but at some point in their training they must also practice on living people. His boss knew his stuff, you had to hand it to him: he actually came up with the impressive diagnosis that Martin's issues could not be *solely* due to a cold. The lack of concentration, the nervousness, the absentmindedness. (As if his ability to concentrate had given up the ghost—ha!) There had to be something else going on.

"Me," I interjected, but unfortunately Martin's boss couldn't hear me.

"Are you having personal problems?" his boss asked.

Martin winced. "Uh, no."

Liar!

"Are you involved in some sort of dispute with someone?"

This was quite an obvious question, of course, given Martin's post-boxing-match face.

"No," Martin said again.

Another lie!

"Do you think you can continue to perform your work in a professional manner?"

At this point Martin should have said no, but instead he said yes.

Yet another lie. There was no way Martin could seriously assume he could. Not if he was at war with me. I had the upper hand, and Martin knew it. But Martin displayed a pride and doggedness that I had not thought him capable of. Although of course his tenacity in absolutely no way presented any kind of obstacle for me. I would break him; of this I didn't have the slightest doubt.

Martin's boss left him alone, and Martin snuck back up the stairwell to his office. I briefly wondered why he never took the elevator, but then as we were going past it the elevator doors opened, giving us a view of a man who wasn't wearing a lab coat but a regular winter coat. A visitor. Only after Martin and I were almost back to his office did I realize who it was: I'd seen him somewhere before. I zoomed back down a floor, but I couldn't find the visitor anywhere. Meanwhile I wasn't sure anymore myself if I hadn't been mistaken. I hesitated for a moment and then whooshed back to Martin.

He was sitting at his computer dictating reports. This report obsession was getting on my nerves. What a boring job. A *dead*-boring job, ha! On the other hand, writing reports struck me as pretty opportune at this particular moment because I could exert a direct influence on them. I waited for him to type a couple of lines. He was commenting on the visible external injuries when he handed the perfect spot to me on a silver platter, describing the head wound as "a calvarial fracture obviously sustained from a blunt object." I supplemented: "We fear rain has been leaking into the poor bastard's braincase."

Martin's upper body, which had been leaning back in his chair, fairly relaxed—or limp, if you will—shot upward. He leaned forward and hammered on the keyboard, deleting my insertion. Such a shame; that would have livened a dry report up a bit for once. Five lines later I inserted a question about what the deal was with the postmortem stab wound that the deceased had sustained to the upper thigh. Same reaction, this time even accompanied by involuntary snorting, like an angry bull. His office mate sitting across from him flashed a furtive glance in Martin's direction.

Martin threw his cool new cordless headset aside, loudly rattled open his desk drawer, seized his old headset, plugged in it, and resumed dictating. His brain was formulating a hateful "na na" before he switched his train of thoughts back off to me in a *tour de force* of will.

Shit.

Without a ghost of a chance at influencing anything, it was suddenly much more boring for me to be present for the laborious genesis and composition of these reports. I was actually looking around for a more riveting form of light entertainment right when the tension in the room suddenly surged. Birgit had entered the room.

"Oh, hello," Martin stammered when he saw her. "This is a surprise."

Not a "nice" surprise, not "what a pleasure to see you," no. Just a surprise. Way not charming.

"I, uh, I happened to be in the neighborhood . . ." Birgit said.

Apparently today was Big Lies Day. No one ever "just happens to be in the neighborhood" of the Institute for Forensic Medicine. There isn't anything around it that would draw in random visitors. It's surrounded by a cemetery and a multilane divided arterial with streetcar tracks down the middle. How bucolic.

"Yes," Martin said, at last standing up, the cord to his old headset catching on some papers, which then tumbled onto the floor.

"Oh," Birgit said, noticing the cord. Then her eyes moved over to the cordless one she had just given him, which in his irritation Martin had just tossed aside someplace an arm's length away. "Someplace" in this case was among the mandarin orange peels on a paper towel at the corner of his desk—ready for the trash, as it were.

"I don't think this was a good idea," Birgit said with tears in her eyes, and then she turned and left.

Martin followed her, and the cord tightened across his throat, shifting the earpiece, which had always been too tight, so it slipped and jabbed his left eye. Martin freed himself from the hopelessly bent contraption and bolted after Birgit. I followed, inconspicuously.

Birgit was already running down the stairs at full speed, Martin and me in tow.

"Birgit," Martin called. "It's not how it looks."

"I don't care," Birgit shouted back over her shoulder.

"I was getting some . . . interference on the cordless headset connection, and some other things going on this morning had already been annoying me, and I was in a rush, and that's why I just quickly plugged the old corded one in again," Martin erupted, a little out of breath.

"That's fine, you can do your work however you want with whatever you want," Birgit said. Her intonation was unambiguously bitchy. I hadn't expected that from her at all, but her pain threshold had obviously been exceeded by this point.

They reached the main floor one right after the other. Birgit went through the glass door into the lobby, letting the door slam shut behind her, and Martin yanked it back open as though he wanted to rip it totally off its hinges.

To the left of us the elevator pinged.

"There's that guy again!" I screamed, extremely agitated.

"What in blazes is wrong now?" Martin roared at the top of his voice.

Birgit swung around and glared at him in stunned horror.

"I didn't mean . . . uh, not you . . ." Martin stammered. The guy from the elevator crossed the lobby and left the building.

"I'm going," Birgit said. "And I'm not sure I ever want to see you again."

Martin stood there thunderstruck, watching her as she left.

"The guy who was just in the corridor. The one who just left. I've seen him somewhere before!" I yelled again.

"Fuck off," Martin thought.

"I can't remember anymore when or where I've seen him. But it's definitely—"

Important, is what I'd wanted to say, but I was interrupted.

"FUCK OFF," Martin repeated more clearly, as though I hadn't understood him correctly the first time.

"Just please go and ask at the reception desk who he was and what he wanted here," I said.

"Go fuck yourself," Martin replied, turning around. He slowly, deflatedly climbed the stairs back up to his office and resumed dictating his reports, but he was so unable to concentrate that half an hour later he packed up his stuff and drove home. I left him alone.

EIGHT

The afternoon was shitty enough, but the night bored me to death. I was wallowing in infinite self-pity, which reached a climax at the darkest hour of the night, around five in the morning. But if I was ever going to be redeemed from my unusual undead existence, then my murder was going to have to be solved; this was one thing I was totally sure of. So I had to swallow my resentment, my personal disappointments, and my self-pity and get Martin to keep going. I thought any hope of this seemed fairly gloomy after the disastrous events of the previous day, but I had to at least try. I waited for him at the Institute with the utmost impatience.

The look on his face shocked me deeply, and it actually should have forewarned me of what other nasty things the day had in store for us, but my mind was on other things. That may have had to do with the fact that a new body had been delivered shortly before Martin's arrival.

Normally the transport casket is brought into the autopsy section, and then two assistants grasp the body, say "one, two, heave," and lift the corpse onto one of the stainless-steel surfaces at the Institute.

Not so in this case. The transport casket arrived, and I hung back a bit as usual since even now looking at the faces of these dead people still depressed me. The assistants then opened the casket, caught their breaths, and then agreed on the sequence: "top first." They didn't even count down, instead saying only "heave ho," and, presto, the torso was neatly unloaded down to the bottom rib on the rib cage, along with the head and arms. The hip and right leg came next, followed by the left leg last.

Of course a corpse doesn't care how many pieces it gets delivered in, but this sight seriously shocked me, so I didn't think to look at the face on the body until much later. Otherwise I would already have been completely beside myself in distress when Martin finally arrived.

He really looked like shit, too; there was no other way to say it. Bloodshot eyes, the bruise on his cheek had morphed into various darker shades of purple and yellowish green, and for the first time since I'd known him his hair wasn't properly combed. His part was totally crooked. I was dismayed.

"Good morning, Martin," I said.

Martin winced, but didn't reply. He went into the break room, poured himself a coffee (!), sat down at his desk, and pulled the cord to his old dictation headset out of the computer. He flung the thing, cord and all, into the drawer, and put on his stylish new headset.

"If you dictate even one single letter into my computer, I will never utter another word to you again, I will bring in an exorcist, and I will spread the most nightmarish gay-sex stories about you," he whispered, noiselessly.

Uh-oh, his tone had clearly sharpened—and yet, he was talking to me again. Sometimes you have to delight in the little things.

"I will be so good you'll wonder what happened to your old friend Pascha," I replied. A snort was his only response.

"Did you talk to Birgit?" I asked.

"That is none of your business," Martin replied.

Well, it looked like the two of us were in for some fun and games today.

Martin went back to work on the interrupted report from yesterday, and I left him in peace. Completely. I didn't talk to him, didn't try to establish contact with him on an emotional level, nothing. I remained downright unseen and unnoticeable. But I was quite near him, watching him. And what I saw worried me. Martin dictated a lot of sentences twice, and others ended abruptly in the middle, although they actually weren't complete sentences at all. He took fairly long pauses to stare out into space or sharpen a pencil down to half its length. He listened to his phone ring for a full minute without really perceiving it, and when colleagues asked him a question or simply wished him a good morning he wouldn't respond until they had repeated themselves for the third time. People were gossiping in the hallway and in the break room, and once again it was all about Martin.

The phone rang again around nine thirty and startled Martin out of his thoughts, so he answered immediately and let his boss talk him into autopsying the *ménage-à-trois* that just came in. We went downstairs.

Even though I still kept a certain distance during autopsies, I really don't feel that uneasy anymore, like I did the first few times. After all, these are dead human beings we're talking about, not zombies, aliens, or slimy critters. Just dead people. Which is why, as I've come to understand in the meantime, forensic pathologists can still pursue their work without losing it, mentally or emotionally. They are investigating human beings who are dead. And interestingly enough, this is how they help these people or their friends and families, although of course they can't bring them back to life again. But they're helping by determining the reason for the death.

In lots of cases it's about life insurance payouts, but more and more frequently it's about medical malpractice lawsuits, or it's about the issue of murder versus not murder.

In the present case all this wasn't so terribly difficult, because whenever you get a person delivered in three parts, the cause of death is relatively clear. However, that's not how forensic pathologists work—we've covered that before. Even when a puzzle like this is lying on the table in front of them, the pathologists always start their exam, and subsequent report, with the clothing, then the scalp including hair, facial skin and facial hair (that is, eyebrows, eyelashes), the fold behind the ear, and things like that. One might think it's excessive to cover such aspects in the case of a torso with the heart dangling out of it from below, a little to the side, but in the present case this assumption would have been rash and incompetent: behind the man's left ear there were dermal abrasions and pressure sores that he had sustained shortly before his death. Presumably a blow from a sap, a kind of homemade weapon, usually a sock filled with sand or lead pellets. So it was possible that the man hadn't thrown himself in front of the regional express train at all but may have been pushed. Another option: he may actually have already been dead before the locomotive's high-quality, German-engineered steel wheels worked their charcuterie.

Of course Martin and his colleague determined all of this totally dispassionately, as usual, but I felt both proud of Martin, who might be solving a brazen murder here disguised as an accident or suicide, and sorry for the dead guy, since I personally thought this kind of serious bodily injury leading to death was almost like being murdered twice. So I looked compassionately into the man's face—and let loose a shriek.

The incision that Martin had just initiated from the throat to the sternum zigzagged. Martin's colleague looked at him with a furrowed brow.

"What is it?" Martin asked me silently. "Are you trying to short-circuit every last one of my nerves?"

"I know that guy," I said in a trembling voice. "I saw him here in the building yesterday. And I recognized him from somewhere, too."

"Recognized, how?" Martin asked in return as his scalpel hovered over the corpse. "Well, who is he then?"

"I don't know," I replied.

Martin moaned so loudly that the expression on his colleague's face turned to one of deep, deep concern.

"If you recognized him, then surely you must know who he is," Martin said.

Martin was right, but not entirely. I racked my brain and, since my thoughts in this case understandably somehow always returned to public transportation, I eventually arrived at the answer:

"I saw him the day I was pushed from the bridge," I said.

"Really?" The question sounded like Martin couldn't decide between incredulity and excitement.

"Yes," I confirmed. "Quite sure."

I very clearly remember that I had seen the tall, dark-haired and dark-complexioned man somewhere after that, too, but I couldn't remember where right now. It would come to me. Now the main thing was to determine the man's identity. And since we knew the guy had been here in the building the day before, we had a high-caliber clue.

"What's wrong, Martin?" his colleague asked, now growing a bit impatient. "Shall we continue?"

"Yes. Uh, no. Well, soon," Martin stammered. "This man has something to do with the Lerchenberg case. You remember, the guy who fell from the bridge . . . And this man was here in the building yesterday."

Martin set his scalpel down on the corpse, peeled his gloves off, and charged out the door.

"Martin," his colleague called after him in shock. "Come back!"

I didn't really understand the fuss, but in the meantime I've learned that you really never, ever interrupt an autopsy. And if you do, then you have to specify a reason for the interruption in your Dictaphone comments, and then you remove and store the body properly and clean the autopsy room and yourself.

Martin apparently forgot all of that, racing through the building as though a snake had bitten him.

"Who was the tall, dark-haired man who was in the building yesterday?" he asked, bursting into the administrative office.

The secretary looked up from her papers, stared in horror at Martin's blood-flecked scrubs, and didn't say anything at all for a moment.

"Please, the man is downstairs," Martin explained, slightly winded. "Dead."

"What?" It sounded more like a shriek of terror than a question.

"The man who was here at the desk yesterday. I saw him in the hallway here," Martin stammered.

"And he's dead?" the secretary asked with tears in her eyes. "That poor man."

"Who is he?" Martin yelled at her.

The door to the director's office opened, and Martin's boss stepped out into his secretary's office. "What is going on here?" he asked, looking with shock at the scene unfolding before him. An unkempt Martin in a splattered surgical gown and a crying secretary staring at each other as though he had threatened her or suggested something lurid.

"Step into my office—" his boss said, and then paused. "Did you come directly from the autopsy room?"

Martin nodded.

"Then please go and take off your gown first and wash your hands—if you haven't done so already."

"But . . ." Martin began.

At that moment his colleague from downstairs joined them in the secretary's office.

"What the hell is going on?" the man asked. "Are we interrupting the autopsy officially now, or are you coming back downstairs?"

The boss's eyes narrowed into slits, and he looked at Martin with growing irritation. Then he turned to Martin's colleague.

"The autopsy is being interrupted," he said. "Please follow the applicable protocol."

The colleague disappeared, Martin trudged back downstairs after him, grumbling, threw his gown into the laundry bin, scrubbed his hands, and went back up to his boss's office.

"What on earth is wrong with you?" the boss asked.

"The dead man we were autopsying downstairs was here in this building yesterday," Martin said, returning to a somewhat steady voice. "I wanted to know what he was doing here and who he is."

"That is not something a professional interrupts an autopsy for," his boss said sternly, the way bosses can get when their employees fuck up.

"In addition, that body is linked to another murder," Martin added defiantly.

"Which murder?"

"Sascha Lerchenberg."

"If I recall correctly, that was not a murder," the boss said.

"Yes, it was. Sascha was pushed," Martin explained. "And shortly before his death, and possibly even after it, he saw that man who is lying downstairs on the table."

"What do you mean, 'and possibly even after it'?" his boss repeated.

Martin realized his error. "Well, you know," he mumbled. "When someone dies and his spirit floats up over the body . . ."

His boss nodded. "You're referring to reports of near-death experiences," the boss coaxed.

Martin nodded.

"But the people who have those are not really dead," the boss said. "They have been to the threshold of death, but they come back to life and can talk about the experience afterward."

Martin nodded.

"But Lerchenberg is dead, isn't he?"

Martin nodded again, although no longer quite as convincingly.

"When would he have been able to make such a statement?" the boss asked. He was wording his questions very carefully.

I could sense the conflicted feelings in Martin. He knew that he could not explain the way things really were to his boss. So he was searching for an explanation that his boss would accept, but he just couldn't find one. His spirit was depleted, exhausted, and he didn't have any creativity left to invent anything. He capitulated.

"He only just now remembered seeing this man again," Martin said. "When he saw the body on the autopsy table."

"About whom are we speaking?" the boss asked.

"Sascha Lerchenberg," Martin mumbled. "Incidentally he goes by 'Pascha.' Although his body is dead, his ghost is buzzing around here in the Institute."

It was dead quiet in the room for rather a long time.

"I hereby approve the leave of absence that you are applying for right now. At least through the end of the week."

"But . . ." Martin's objection was only mild.

"No buts," his boss made clear. "If you want to extend your leave on Monday, then that will also be approved. But on condition that you go and visit the Counseling Services Unit."

Martin nodded.

"I'll get the paperwork ready. Please stop back by here on your way home and sign it," his boss said, standing up. He patted Martin on the shoulder. "Get yourself a little rest," he said, sounding friendly but concerned. "Get a few good nights' sleep, take some walks, go out to dinner with someone."

Martin nodded.

"And please take only the most important things with you from your office."

We crept back to Martin's desk. Martin collapsed into his chair, put the cordless headset back on, and stared into space for a moment. Then he lapsed back into a frenzy of activity, waking his computer back up with a voice command, accessing the internal forensics database, and printing the photo of the dead man that he had taken at the start of the autopsy and saved nice and proper under—for want of the actual name—the ID number along with the date and time. Then he opened his dictation program. But before he could get blabbing, Katrin burst into his office saying, "Have you heard? That good-looking guy from yesterday who came in wanting to arrange international transportation to bring his sister's body back home? Now he's dead, too. Run over by a train."

Martin looked at her as though he were only just now waking up.

"His sister?" he asked.

"Yes, that anonymous body who died from anaphylactic shock," Katrin said. She was suddenly talking the way you do to a child who's a bit slow.

"What's the man's name?" Martin asked.

"Sjubek Laringosch," Katrin replied without hesitating but rolling the R nicely. "Sounds mysterious, huh? It's Moldovan."

"Moldovan?" Martin asked back. "The guy is . . ."

"Yes, from the far-flung regions of Eastern Europe that the EU has not yet assimilated and that reject the blessings of both standardized European condom sizing and even the euro itself, which I understand people are now calling the yoyo," Katrin confirmed, batting her eyes and smiling. "A well-hewn representative of a mysterious steppe people, with eyes as shiny and black as the polished obsidian of a signet ring." She sighed and became serious. "At least, that's what I thought yesterday. Today he's just some poor bastard who committed suicide far away from home, presumably consumed by grief for his dead sister."

"Murdered," Martin said absentmindedly. "Not a suicide."

"Sorry?" Katrin asked. "Murder?"

Martin nodded. "What was the sister's name?" he asked.

"Semira," Katrin said. "I was actually surprised that he would come to the Institute at all and open himself up to trouble with the police just so he could bury his sister appropriately back in Moldova, only then to throw himself under a train. It doesn't make sense somehow."

"What was his trouble with the police?" Martin asked.

"He doesn't have a visa or an entry stamp in his passport."

"What does that mean?" Martin asked. His brain was really light-years away from its normal performance level.

"He's here illegally, and I assume not just since yesterday," Katrin said.

Martin's boss popped in through the door. "Dr. Gänsewein, I have signed your application here."

Martin silently stood up, removed his headset, took the paperwork, added his signature to the bottom, and grabbed his duffle coat.

"See you," he said, and he left the office without turning around once.

"This is great! Now that you've got some time off, you'll have more time for the investigation," I said on our way to the car.

Martin's response left much to be desired: he didn't respond at all.

"I've been giving some thought to the best way for us to proceed," I said. "I think we should resume our investigation by focusing on Semira."

"The police will do that; we don't need to get involved," Martin murmured.

"But they aren't going to come up with anything," I said.

We were already sitting in the trash can, but Martin showed no signs of turning the ignition.

"The detectives on the case—or to be more precise, my friend Gregor—have apparently also been told that I was walking around door to door the other night, showing people a drawing and telling some completely wacked story that I assume absolutely no one believes."

"Yes, but we were on the trail of something completely different then," I said impatiently.

"And the police *were* able to figure out where that woman lived," he hastened to add.

"Also something completely different," I said even more impatiently.

"I see," Martin said, and I thought he sounded a bit sarcastic.

"First of all, the bouncer was a rat who didn't pass on any relevant information about Semira's identity, just an observation to his control officer in the police."

Martin winced when I said "control officer," but I didn't let him mull that over at all. "Plus, now we're trying to get hold of information that it is a crime to even know, information about an illegal immigrant. No one can pass that information on to the police here because then you'd be admitting to harboring an illegal."

Martin had to take a moment to think about that as he started his trash can's toy engine. God, that sound totally makes the hair on the back of my neck stand up. Spectrally, of course.

"Why are you so convinced that the woman has any significance in this case?" Martin asked.

"Well, because she comes from the East," I said. How was it that Martin hadn't gotten this yet?

As expected, he lived up to my worst fears and asked: "From the East?"

OK, just between us: Martin's mental potency has degraded dramatically over the past few days. I'm not sure what's been causing it exactly, but the trend has started worrying me. He's been acting like some blond bimbo who you want to explain the theory of relativity to, but who doesn't get that time isn't merely what passes while her nail polish dries.

"Pay attention," I began, trying to lay out the Big Picture for Martin in lots of tiny, manageable baby steps. "It started when I stole a car."

"It isn't certain whether that event triggered subsequent developments or whether it just coincidentally occurred a few days before you died. In fact, if I understand correctly, this was just one of hundreds of previous car thefts," Martin threw in.

Well, I stood corrected. The degradation was not in his mental potency in general. Apparently he could still reflect on things theoretically. What had degraded was his ability to appreciate the brutality and affliction of living and dying in the real world. Was his telling me this supposed to give me hope now?

"While it is true that I've pinched plenty of cars in my time, never an SLR and never one with a body in the trunk," I replied as dispassionately as possible, trying to sound objectively cool and logical.

"OK," Martin relented. I was slowly getting the impression that his mental lethargy was abating. I always say work limits human development, and this forced leave of absence was already starting to show its healing effect.

"So," I began again. "I steal a car with a body in it, a couple of days later I feel like someone is following me, and then I get pushed off a bridge. At the time I didn't consciously register him, but since then I've grown pretty sure that I did see the Bulgarian or whatever he is multiple times during the last two days of my earthly life."

"Uh-huh."

"OK. So then, Semira's body was missing for a few days and then it shows up with signs that animals had started eating it, indicating that she had been unloaded somewhere in the woods," I continued.

Martin nodded.

"At first no one can identify the woman, and then suddenly her brother pops up—he's the guy I recognized—to transport her home for a proper burial, and then the next day that same guy is lying dead himself in the freezer downstairs."

Martin thought for another moment and then asked: "What does that have to do with Eastern Europe?"

"The stolen cars get sent to Eastern Europe, which also happens to be where our dead Hänsel and Gretel here come from."

"OK," Martin said. "So who is the murderer? Count Dracula?"

I gave a loud moan. He wasn't taking me seriously.

"I don't know who the murderer is," I said. "But for me there is a clear connection between the car theft, the body in the SLR, and this most recent murder. I don't know any more, which is why I need you so that we can find out the rest."

"I don't feel like finding it out," Martin said. "I want to make up with Birgit, get my job back, and get rid of you." He thought for a moment. "But not in that order," he added.

Asshole.

"Do you think you can get either your job or Birgit back as long as this series of murders hasn't been solved?" I asked.

Martin was thinking about that, I could tell, but he was able to keep his precise train of thought a secret from me. These thoughts were undoubtedly not very heartening, since his mood was darkening more and more.

"There is only one way for you to redeem your reputation as an impotent crackpot with Birgit and as a psychologically unstable scalper with your boss: you've got to prove to them all that your incoherent drivel wasn't crazy talk and that you knew more from the get-go than the others did. Because I told you."

"I'll never speak to another living soul about you," Martin said. "It doesn't matter how many crimes of the century I might solve—there is no one in the world who will believe this story."

"Then sideline me," I relented, although I was pretty sure that he would end up breaking his vow. "But solve the crimes. Otherwise, your reputation will be permanently ruined."

He thought again, this time for quite a while, all the way until we reached the door to his apartment.

"And what do you suggest I do next?" Martin asked.

I had him where I wanted him.

"We've got to figure out who owns the SLR," I said.

"Terrific idea," Martin said, caustically. "Unfortunately no cars of that make and model have been reported stolen, so that might be a tad bit difficult, don't you think?"

"Semira will help us," I said. "The woman was a whore, and whores have johns. That's how we'll track him down."

Martin opened the door to his apartment, took off his shoes, arranged them neatly side by side, hung the duffle coat up without any creases on its hook, and went into the kitchen to make himself some tea.

"We'll get going at eight o'clock," he said. "Until then I want some peace and quiet."

I promised him heaven and earth that I'd stay clear of him, and he parked me in front of the TV to watch talk show after talk show and soap opera after soap opera until night finally came and we resumed our investigational tour.

———•———

This time the milieu we were looking into was richer.

It still had to do with sex for sale, but not the cheap sex you buy off the street and receive on the street. We were moving into the environment Semira fit into, based on her neighbor's description. Pricey. Martin had intentionally grabbed his long, dark winter coat from the closet, the one he'd bought for his father's funeral and had never worn again since. At least in this coat he wouldn't immediately look like he'd taken a wrong turn and was ringing the bell to politely ask for directions.

We had the drawing of Semira with us, hoping we could get the information we needed from one of her colleagues. It was clear that this wouldn't be an inexpensive excursion, because the first thing a man is offered in an upscale "nail salon," as it were, isn't sex—but alcohol. At a price that even the Yanks during Prohibition would have deemed a rip-off.

The first problem with our plan was that it turned out Martin wasn't actually familiar with even one whorehouse. How were we supposed to comb the appropriate body-rub parlors if we didn't know where they are? So, I had to draw on my bad memory, even though I'd never set foot in one of these upscale riding stables; I had never gotten flush enough during my short life to afford one. But, of course, even in my crowd people are familiar with certain addresses. Definitely not all of them, but we didn't have time for all of them, anyway. We just had to hope that we were looking in the right area. Had Semira owned a car? Presumably not, because the neighbor hadn't mentioned anything about that. Of course, someone might have driven her to work and home again, or she might have taken any of the numerous transportation options offered by the Cologne Transit Authority . . . hmm, now that's more my kind of metrosexual.

But, again, we restricted our search to the radius of what Semira could have reached by foot, also because we didn't feel like wandering aimlessly back and forth through the whole city. And within her walking radius were some of the Russian tochkas, at which establishments the term "Russian" is used for simplicity's sake to refer to anyone born east of Berlin. Not entirely politically correct, but easy to remember.

So Martin stopped at the ATM first, withdrew cash up to his limit, and then parked his trash can on an inconspicuous residential street near our hunting ground.

Brothel I, Scene 1—lights, camera, action: The door opens, the doorman waves Martin in. Red ultraplush. Lots of loud people of presumably Eastern European origin wearing lots of gold on their wrists, necks, fingers, and teeth.

Martin approaches the bar, orders a beer. Looks around. Much too conspicuously, and I tell him so.

"How else am I supposed to look around?" he asks.

"Inconspicuously," I say.

"With my eyes shut, or what?" he grumbles.

We haven't even been working for ten minutes, and already Martin's getting cantankerous. I think we're in for some fun and games.

———•———

I don't want to bore you with every last detail of our procession through the big-city cathouses, because most of them were neither exciting nor stimulating, just sucky and boring. The interior designers in this industry tend toward a surprisingly uniform ultraplush décor, varying only in the shade—lighter or darker red, with an occasional foray into purple or orange. Martin always sat at the bar, he always ordered a beer that he hardly drank, he always waited for a woman to sit next to him, and he always steered the conversation toward Semira.

"You can call me Semira if you'd like," was the standard response, cooed and not spoken.

"I'm looking for a specific Semira," Martin answered with equal consistency. "This one here."

The business with the drawing was an extremely delicate matter, because the operators of such houses keep a watchful eye on men who behave oddly and give the impression they're looking to buy something other than love. Martin got kicked out on his ass twice after showing the drawing; after that he got more careful.

Nonetheless, most of the reactions were not the one we were hoping for. No recognition, no additional information. Not to mention that lots of the ladies Martin spoke to had only very limited command of the German language.

Including the tiny blonde who looked like the reason she hadn't made the cut for the latest James Bond casting call was probably her size: on screen she'd have looked like a hot face on a stick next to any of the hunks who'd had the honor of playing the cocky British spy. She was at least six centimeters shorter than even average height, but she dominated the bar the moment she entered it. She had not only a smoking-hot body that you could clearly see in several places through the outfit she had on. But she also had the whitest, nicest teeth that ever achieved fame in any toothpaste ad and the brightest violet eyes that have ever shone upon a male. If I'd been Martin's cardiologist, I'd have been extremely concerned about his chances of survival at this moment. His pulse ceased briefly, only to start thundering against his ribs again so hard that I thought I could make out the collar of his coat thumping with each heartbeat.

She sat down on the barstool next to Martin, looked at his glass of beer that had gone flat, and then looked at Martin.

"Two champagnes," he ordered without missing even a single beat.

Meanwhile I found my seat in the curve of the B-girl's neck, enjoying the view down her neckline toward her lap, which was only unsubstantially covered by a tiny little sheer skirt.

"What wish can I make come true for you today?" the angelic being asked.

Martin swallowed the half glass of bubbles in one gulp after clinking glasses with her.

"I have an obscure wish," he stammered. He had to start again twice before getting the sentence out fully and error-free.

"You're in luck," she said, laying her hand on Martin's. "Today I'm making even obscure wishes come true."

She smiled warmly. Not all frumpy, like lots of others, not with euro signs in her eyes, not tired—no, she smiled warmly. Cheerfully. Radiantly.

Martin was taking his time. Maybe he was unable to do it any other way. Maybe he was just in another dimension, caught in an unearthly plane not subject to time reckoning. Anyways, he didn't say anything for a long time, sipping on the champagne he had left and staring at this delightful creature.

"What does your obscure wish look like, then?" she asked at some point. "Or would you prefer to tell me tête-à-tête?"

I could see an unambiguous YES starting to materialize in Martin's brain, so I yelled, "Stop!"

"What?" he asked me gruffly.

"If you say yes now, it'll be very, very expensive," I said.

"Hmm," Martin mumbled.

"And think of Birgit," I hastened to add.

"Birgit . . ."

I realized that Martin wasn't actually thinking of having sex with this vision of a woman at all; he just wanted to keep staring into her eyes and talking with her.

"Dude, that little charmer sitting on the stool in front of you is a whore," I said. "She wants to blow you off or . . . whatever else."

Martin swallowed and suddenly found his feet back on the ground, briefly wondered how expensive the champagne he'd ordered was, and then he said his line: "I'm looking for a friend."

He nonchalantly held the drawing out to the angel so she could see it.

"Semira!" She almost yelled it, but she quickly put her hand over her mouth, opened her blue eyes wide, and stared at Martin, taken aback. "What's happened to her? She and I had plans to go out, but she stood me up, and that's not like her at all."

Martin's heart, which had only just started easing its pace, started pounding harder again.

"Did she work here?" he asked.

The blonde shook her head. "You're—not a customer of hers?"

Now Martin shook his head, but of course not half as gracefully.

"Is it OK if we keep talking here?" he asked carefully, looking around. Several sinister-looking guys were watching the two of them.

"Oh," the angel said, sliding down from her stool. "For us it's OK, but it's bad for business. Come with me."

So Martin slid down off his stool, too, and the bartender subtly reminded him it was fine for him to leave—but his sixty euros for the beer and two glasses of champagne should stay behind. Martin paid and followed the blonde outside.

"So, where do you know Semira from?" she asked. "And what do you want from her?"

"I don't want anything from her," Martin said. "She's dead."

"No!" she gasped, tears filling her enormous eyes. "How?"

"Anaphylactic shock," Martin said. "That means . . ."

"I know what it is," the blonde hissed. Uh-oh, the kitty cat was extending her claws. "And who are you?" she asked.

"Martin Gänsewein. Coroner."

He offered his hand, and she reflexively shook it and whispered, "Yvonne Kleinewefers."

Honestly, I couldn't make head or tail of what was happening here. I was slowly starting to wonder how the blonde fit into this story. She wasn't your typical lady of the night at a Russian tochka. If she were, she wouldn't have been allowed to leave the establishment with a customer during working hours. Martin was having similar thoughts, plus he was starting to get cold, so he suggested the nearest place.

"There's a café over there. Why don't we get something warm to drink?"

She nodded and followed him.

Martin ordered a chamomile tea, which they didn't have, a peppermint tea, which they also didn't have, and before he could further display his in-depth knowledge of other monastery-grown teas and tisanes, Ms. Kleinewefers ordered two coffees. *Basta.*

She also took over the conversation, like a celestial being that had metamorphosed from a tinsel angel to an avenging angel.

"What has happened that would send a coroner through the brothels at night asking questions about Semira?" she asked.

"Didn't you see Semira's picture in the newspaper?" Martin asked as a counter-maneuver.

"No, after my nighttime fieldwork and daytime course-work I don't have terribly much time left over to practice bourgeois self-edification by reading newspapers," she hissed.

"Fieldwork?" Martin asked, irritated.

"I'm doing my master's thesis on the expectations of men who go to brothels. What they're really looking for there, their genuine needs, which don't necessarily always have to do with sex but which they would like fulfilled," she rattled out. "My adviser is not really all that sold on it, which is why I've been gathering material for some time so that he will approve the topic."

"You're doing a master's in psychology?" Martin asked.

"No, economics."

Martin took a sip of his coffee, which had just arrived at the table. "Are you trying to put one over on me?" he asked between two coughing fits.

"Ever since Germany legalized prostitution, it's become a more and more important source of revenue the government can now legally line its pockets with. Even beautiful Cologne with its world-famous cathedral has been levying a 'pleasure tax' since 2004, which brings in just under a million euros a year."

"A sex tax?" Martin stammered. "What, from the . . ." Evidently his well-cultivated vocabulary was failing him here.

"From the whores, pimps, and bordellos. The tax administration doesn't care who pays, but a portion of each euro earned in this service industry ends up in the treasury."

Martin shook his head, speechless.

"Since prostitution is legal now, the Federal Employment Agency can also theoretically find a job placement for an unemployed woman at a brothel now. No one has actually made a placement like that yet, however."

"Not yet," Martin mumbled.

"Well, within that context, the question arises how to optimize supply within this very lucrative service industry. As I'm sure you know, expanding services is the future."

"And you got to know Semira through this, uh, fieldwork?" Martin asked.

She shook her head. "The other way around. I got to know Semira at the university."

"She was a student?" Martin was getting more and more confused. "But she wasn't even legally in this country . . ."

"But she was damned smart. She wasn't registered, so she couldn't attend small seminars. But she could attend the large lectures where there are hundreds of students. At a giant university with umpteen thousand students no one notices if the lecture hall is missing a student or has one extra."

Yvonne had been stirring her coffee the whole time and only now realized she hadn't even added any sugar to it yet. She remedied this quickly, then took a big gulp.

"Although she was very cautious and didn't actually want to make friends with anyone at all, not even other students, we sat next to each other a couple of times and got to talking. She told me that she worked as a call girl. That's how I picked the topic for my thesis."

"Did she work for an agency, or freelance?" Martin asked.

"For an agency. Or rather, for an agent. I'd have liked to interview him, but she never told me who he is."

"Then do you know how she originally met this agent?" Martin asked.

"Only that it was more or less a coincidence, because his main line of business is actually something else. 'High-end luxury,' I remember how she worded it exactly. Semira was proud that the guy described her as a luxury product, too. Personally I don't think being classified as a 'product' is a compliment."

"Too bad," Martin said. "Without the agent we're pretty much groping in the dark."

"You still haven't explained to me what you're doing here," Yvonne said.

"Yes, well, that's also a bit complicated," Martin said.

That wasn't cutting it with Yvonne, which she made more than clear by raising an eyebrow.

"Semira did die from anaphylactic shock, but this apparently happened in the course of her professional practice," Martin began.

Nicely worded. And he stated it totally seriously—with scientific precision, really.

"I suspect the client she was with when she died put her into the trunk of his car in order to secretly spirit the body away. Unfortunately it was an especially valuable car, and unfortunately the car was then stolen. With Semira's body in the trunk."

"No!" Yvonne blurted out. "It's like in a movie!"

"Yes," Martin agreed. "It seems that two other recent murders have also been committed in connection with this regrettable death, a car thief and Semira's brother."

"Oh my God, it just gets worse and worse!" she gasped.

"Which is why I need to find out who the owner of the stolen car is," Martin said.

Yvonne furrowed her brow and contemplated him for a moment, shaking her head. "But why are you sitting around here in the middle of the night trying to find out who the owner is in such a complicated way? The police must surely be able to do that with the press of a button."

"That would require knowing the license plate number," Martin said.

"If the car was so extraordinarily valuable as you say, then it's not like there will be thousands and thousands of them. Surely it must be possible to get a list of the owners."

Boy oh boy, this one was really sharp as a tack. Even though she was blonde.

Martin hemmed and hawed. "The police have not yet made . . . certain connections," he finally said.

A short pause as our little goldfinch did some serious brooding.

"So you're out here on your own, then?" Yvonne asked.

Martin nodded.

"Good for you," she mumbled. "And because you can't get hold of the list of people who own this model of car from the police, you have to track down Semira's clients and find the one she was with last?"

Martin nodded, relieved that someone was finally thinking along the same lines as him and didn't think he was batshit crazy. However, she didn't know even half of the whole story. About me, for instance.

"Let me see what I can do to help you further," she said pensively. "The agent's name would be great, but I don't know it. I don't know Semira's clients' names, either, of course, since she was very discreet. But she definitely made a few comments that might help us."

She thought some more and noisily slurped on her coffee.

"Did she have, uh, I mean, well . . . in what circumstances did she die?" Yvonne asked.

"She was naked when she died, and she had recently had sexual intercourse," Martin explained very objectively. As far as his reports go, Martin was master of his domain. "She had eaten a hazelnut cookie before or after the sexual intercourse, which triggered her allergic reaction."

"Protected or unprotected sex?" Yvonne asked.

"Unprotected. But with lubricant, which is why I assumed it was with a client."

"That stupid girl," Yvonne mumbled. "I'm sorry, I shouldn't speak ill of the dead. But she knew exactly how dangerous sex without a condom is, but she still had clients she didn't use one with. I always told her . . ." Yvonne wiped her eyes.

"She was, uh, healthy," Martin said. "No sexually trans-mitted diseases, no HIV. She apparently knew which clients she did and didn't need a condom with."

"Evidence of handcuff use?" Yvonne asked.

"None," Martin said. "No use of force, no fetish-related practices, no drugs."

She summed the main points up again: "So we're look-ing for someone who has an unusual car, hires a call girl, has unprotected sex with her, isn't into any kinky games, and who gave her hazelnut cookies that she died from."

"Correct."

We let her have some time to mull that over; Martin drank his coffee and ordered two more.

"I can remember comments about two clients that might be worth considering," Yvonne said with the fresh cup of coffee in front of her.

Martin leaned forward eagerly.

"The one guy she used to call 'Dr. Strangelove' . . ."

"She gave her clients nicknames?" Martin asked, amazed.

I snickered. What nickname would Martin have gotten?

"Well, sure," Yvonne said. "I wanted to know as much as possible about what her clients wanted, but she didn't want to name names. So we had to find a way to easily but dis-creetly talk about the men."

Martin nodded.

"So, to continue, Dr. Strangelove is an entrepreneur, something to do with steel, I think. He has at least four fancy cars, including a Porsche and a Jaguar. He's a widower, and harbors an abysmally deep mistrust of women—he thinks they are all only interested in his money."

"That's probably true, too," I interjected, but Martin didn't acknowledge me.

"He has two grown daughters who keep trying to set him up with women, but for them he plays the monk. He satisfies his urges with call girls, and over the last two years exclusively with Semira." She thought for a moment. "At least he said he was exclusive with her."

"Yes," Martin said thoughtfully. "That might well be something to take with a grain of salt. Does he live in Cologne?"

"I think so, yes."

Meanwhile Martin had taken out a pen and a piece of paper from the pocket of his jacket, jotting down the most important information.

"The other guy she used to call 'Il Papa.'"

Martin wrote down "Il Papa."

"He's married, but he told Semira his wife is frigid and unapproachable. He doesn't actually live in Cologne, but he comes to town a lot on business, so he rents a small apartment here."

"What does he do?" Martin asked.

Yvonne shook her head. "I don't know."

"What did he want from Semira?" Martin asked.

Stupid question, I thought. Sex, of course.

"Warmth?" Yvonne said.

Female mumbo jumbo, I thought.

"Sex of course, too," she said.

All right!

"But he only wanted a little sex, and otherwise just lots of cuddling. Warmth that he wasn't getting from his wife anymore."

Why would the man tell Semira such bullshit, I wondered. Normal men have to tell women baloney like that so they'll jump into bed with them. But a call girl will jump anyway, so why all the claptrap?

"How did she come up with the nicknames?" Martin asked. "Why was one called Dr. Strangelove and the other Il Papa?"

Yvonne shrugged. "No idea. I asked her that too, but she said only that the nicknames suited them. She didn't want to give any explanation for them so no one could guess the men's identities."

"Too bad," I said. "After all, that's exactly what we want."

Meanwhile the supply of coffee had gone dry again, and Yvonne gave such a big yawn that she almost fell out of her chair. They exchanged phone numbers, Martin paid, Yvonne decided to take a taxi home, and we cruised homeward in the sardine can. Martin crashed into bed and slept nine and half hours straight. I watched TV until I couldn't stand what was on anymore, and then I moved to the kitchen—after all, I didn't have any eyelids that I might mercifully have closed, and I couldn't turn off the tube, either. A few days ago I was desperate because I couldn't switch the thing on, and now it was the opposite. Life sure is strange, especially when you're dead.

———————

After a proper tea, a little bowl of sugar-free muesli, and a shower, the next morning Martin was feeling fit enough to continue the investigation. I felt beat and was grumpy because I had no idea how to proceed. Dr. Strangelove and Il Papa were phantoms (actually I had wanted to say they were as hard to detect as cum stains on a shower curtain, but I've been making serious strides toward improving my language here) who turned up in stories, or who killed people but left no evidence you could trace back to them, but Martin was of an entirely different view.

"We have one clue as to where we have to go to search for the two of them," Martin said.

"Where?" I replied in a huff.

"Where you stole the car," he said with satisfaction.

"Great," I said. "Then let's stroll down to the Cologne Congress Centre that thousands of people go in and out of every day and ask whether Dr. Strangelove or Il Papa may have heard one of the numerous presentations or attended any seminars on that illustrious day."

Martin could not be dissuaded by my bad mood.

"We're going to find out what events were being held that day, and then we'll decide what direction to go next."

"And what direction would that be?" I asked.

"If there was a presentation for entrepreneurs, say, that might give us a clue about Dr. Strangelove," Martin said. "We might even be able to find an employee who remembers an attendee with that unusual car."

The idea wasn't totally stupid, I had to admit. And the likelihood was not exactly remote that a pimply trainee banquet server would have found out about a rocket ship like our SLR being parked out in the lot. People always go and take a look at nice rides, and some pompous guy who works there will always know who it belongs to . . . Hmm, maybe we really were going to be able to find out the owner's identity this way. The owner who presumably murdered me! I got hot and cold at the idea.

We ran back through all the details of the information we had about the two men in question: Dr. Strangelove had to be strange in some way, although we didn't know if his name referred to how he looked or something else. He was an entrepreneur involved somehow in steel. He had several cars. He lived in Cologne, was a widower, and had two grown daughters, so he had to be at least forty, maybe even fifty or older.

Il Papa was married, stayed in Cologne only in a second apartment because he had business here. Maybe his nickname had to do with getting on in years. Maybe Semira christened him that just because he called her "my child" or something; we just didn't know. Maybe he was Italian *and* an old fart *and* he called her "my child." No idea. We'd have to keep our eyes and ears open. *Vámonos.*

On the way we were still thinking about what reason to give for asking about the events that had been held on the illustrious day, but after batting around a few ideas and not being able to agree on anything remotely believable, Martin ended the conversation with a wave of his hand.

"We'll just act like it's the most normal thing in the world to ask about past events, and we won't give any reason."

No sooner said than done—but it didn't work.

"May I ask why you need this information?" the pretty receptionist asked in her pretty short-skirt suit with her pretty smile on her pretty face. Martin blinked stupidly at her.

"It has to do with an inquiry into a death," he said after a brief moment. He whipped out his business card, held it out for the pretty little mouse to read, but pulled it away again when she reached for it.

"Shouldn't the police be handling the investigation?" she asked cautiously.

"No problem," Martin said with a friendly smile, looking only the tiniest bit pinched. "If you'd like to have the police come out, I can arrange that with a single phone call. We—that is, the investigative team I'm part of and I—were thinking it would be somewhat more discreet for you if I just popped in here quickly for the information. It was easy for me to stop by because you're on my way to my next appointment, you see."

He pulled his cell phone out of his pocket.

"Um—wait a second," she said.

She vanished into the office behind the counter and reappeared two minutes later with a few still-warm sheets of printer paper.

"Here you are."

Martin briefly looked through the papers, tucked them into his pocket, nodded at her, and walked back to the trash can, which was parked around the corner. With a car like that you simply cannot park right in front of a convention center and *not* attract attention.

We got into the trash can and read through the printout. It's positively dreadful what all topics people hold conventions on. "Feminizing the World Experience of Preschool and Elementary School Children" was a symposium with a panel discussion by some association of preschool teachers.

We didn't expect either Dr. Strangelove or Il Papa to be among the preschool teachers. So we kept reading.

"*Traduttore, Traditore:* Language Professionals' Self-Conception between Taking Sides and Risking Lives." Hmm. Translators, right? Maybe interpreters? We lacked both certitude and mutual agreement, but nonetheless the two of us shared a rather gloomy expectation of finding the friend we sought amid the illustrious world of polyglots.

Although Il Papa did sound quite Italian . . . But we decided to keep looking for now.

"Germany as a Place for Business: Is Globalization Passing Us By?" Woo hoo, that sounded promising. Could our steel entrepreneur Dr. Strangelove be interested in globalization? Martin added a checkmark. Truly a systematic person. We continued through the list.

The "Annual Meeting of Speechwriters" didn't inspire us, and with a snort Martin dismissed the "Christian Lifestyle League: Uncompromising Action in a Society in Moral Decline."

"I actually do consider myself a Christian," he said, "and I even dutifully pay my church tax. But if 'uncompromising action' means forgoing organ transplants or medically necessary procedures because they desecrate the inviolability of the person, to say nothing of wanting to ban forensic medicine to avoid disturbing the dead . . ."

He interrupted himself mid-sentence, which is not at all like him, and he gaped at the paper, which he was holding perfectly still as though he were playing jackstraws and feared losing if he so much as twitched.

"Have you turned into a pillar of salt there, speaking of being a good Christian?" I asked, proud that I was able to leverage one of the two stories from the Bible I know. The other is the one with the ark. I always liked that one a lot. Two of every sort, then everybody gets the boat rocking by screwing until the sun comes out. What a great image.

"Christian," Martin whispered. Was he lost in some kind of religious trance? Or was he just engaged in some intense reflection? I couldn't make out any supernatural waves, so I cleared my throat loud and clear.

No reaction.

"What now?" I asked after a while, hoping my words would get me further than coughing.

"Dr. Eilig," Martin mumbled.

"No, Dr. Strangelove," I said, correcting him. Was he getting all mixed up now, already?

"No," he said. "There is a Bundestag representative whose name is Dr. Christian Eilig."

"Ah ha," I said. Active listening. We covered that before, remember?

"He's against organ transplants, and lately he's come out against autopsies, too," Martin said.

"Rings a bell," I said, because I vaguely recalled some discussion along those lines in the break room at the Institute.

"The guy is more Catholic than the Pope," Martin said.

Stupid saying, never liked it. Plus, I didn't understand why Martin was making such a pregnant pause right now, of all times. Sometimes it's pretty annoying that I never went to college.

"Um, what are you trying to tell me?" I asked, slightly irritated.

"Il Papa," Martin said. "That's Italian. It means 'the Pope.'"

"You're not trying to tell me that the Pope was there?" I asked.

"No. But Dr. Eilig was."

"And?" I said. I could certainly understand Martin getting into a tizzy about this guy drawing his whole profession into question, but we were right in the middle of a murder investigation, and we had much better things to do than ponder the latest lunacies that some wingnut had brought up two weeks ago at the convention center.

"Dr. Christian Eilig, or 'Dr. Christian' for short, is more Catholic than the Pope, as they say; he lives in a nice area out past Bergisch Gladbach in the hills east of Cologne, but as anyone who reads the local papers here knows, he has an apartment in town from which he has a view of Cologne Cathedral. And, he collects cars."

"Matchbox?" I asked Martin.

"No, real ones," Martin replied. "When asked about this vice, he says, 'Everyone has to have a vice, otherwise we'd all be saints, not people.'"

Hmm.

"In addition, he's married."

I'd have liked to nod pensively, but that wasn't possible, obviously, so I said hmm again.

"Are you thinking what I'm thinking?" Martin asked.

"I think so," I said. "How do we find out if the Pope had an SLR?" I asked.

"The newspaper," Martin said. "If the Pope is driving an SLR, they'll know about it."

He took out his cell phone, dialed a number he knew by heart, and then gave his name and mentioned "coroner's office."

"No, we haven't got any interesting bodies right now, at least not on my end," he said apparently in response to a question. "This time I've actually got a non-business-related question, if that's all right. I've found myself in a silly bet with someone, and I'm hoping you can confirm that I won."

He listened for a moment and then laughed. "All right, does Dr. Eilig, a.k.a. Dr. Christian, own a Mercedes SLR?"

Martin's face grew long. "No? Are you sure?" The corners of his mouth that had sunk down in disappointment suddenly shot up.

"Are you sure? Wow, I'm so relieved."

He laughed again, promised to keep sending official press releases to the e-mail address he already had, and hung up.

"That guy is a freelancer over at the *Cologne Advertiser*, and he owes me various favors," Martin explained with a very satisfied expression on his face. I was amazed because I hadn't at all expected Martin to keep an account like that. Once again I'd been completely wrong about him, and once again he'd surprised me. I was going to have to start getting used to the idea that people can be complex and interesting even outside the environment I'd been hanging out in the past few years. It's actually kind of exciting to see the world this way. Even women here weren't just bed bunnies but human beings, with intellect and personality. OK, I wasn't quite that far yet, but hanging around with Martin had started to open my mind up to all kinds of new possibilities.

"Eilig did have an SLR, but it hasn't been seen for about ten days. After a reporter had asked him about it three days ago, he said he'd gotten an excellent offer for the car from a prospective buyer abroad, and he sold it to him."

"Well now all my warning lights are flashing," I said.

"Exactly," Martin said, his voice squeaking with excitement. "We got him." He said it aloud. And he said it again: "We got the bastard."

NINE

We drove to Eilig's address in Cologne, which Martin had elicited from another reporter so no one would notice his sudden interest in the man. His apartment was one of six in the building, each seventy square meters according to the poster in front advertising the two empty units. These were condos, actually, but that didn't surprise us. If the arrangement of the doorbells and nameplates matched the arrangement of the apartments, then Eilig's apartment was on the second floor on the right. Martin positioned the car in front of the entry while I orbited the building and got a marvelous view through the gigantic wall of glass into the living room where Eilig was sitting in a deep leather armchair staring into space. Strictly speaking he was staring at the flat-screen TV hanging on the wall in his line of sight, but the TV was turned off, and I didn't think that Eilig was staring at the dark glossy rectangle.

In his left hand he was holding a glass with three melting ice cubes in it. Either the guy was missing his car with a longing that really made you feel sorry for him, or else he had another problem. I was already inclined toward the latter analysis, even before seeing him like this. But if you watched the call girl you hired to brighten your mood die in agony, and then you decided you needed to spirit her body away without anyone noticing, and to do that you had to abuse the coolest fucking car in the world, only to have someone steal your rocket ship complete with the body in the trunk, then I'm thinking you've got a pretty good reason to feel melancholic. But then if on top of that you also needed to murder the car thief to keep even his dying words from publicly disclosing the corpse in the trunk, then from my perspective that would be reason enough to be staring into space with a drink in your hand. Eilig apparently thought so, too. He didn't stir.

I reported my observations to Martin, and he was pleased Eilig was home. He was less interested in everything else.

I whooshed back to the living room window and stopped in horror. The chair was empty. After a moment's terror I saw Eilig standing over by the bookcase. He was just hanging up the phone. He turned around, picked up an attaché case from next to the armchair, and walked out of the living room.

I raced back to Martin and updated him on my surveillance just as the red warning light started blinking at the entrance to the ramp leading down to the underground garage. A Jag with tinted windows exited. We couldn't tell who the driver was, but we both automatically assumed Eilig was sitting in the car, and we followed him. In the trash can. Fortunately traffic was heavy, and we were hitting all red lights instead of green, so our little pedal car was actually able to keep up in the car "chase."

Eilig wasn't concentrating on his driving, which may have been due to any number of causes, not the least of which was indubitably a certain blood alcohol level, if you recall the glass with the ice cubes. As we followed him we enjoyed some excited speculation. Where was he driving to? And why? At first we thought he was driving to his local parliamentary office since he had an attaché case with him, but he wasn't driving in the right direction for that. Then he started getting closer to the neighborhood where Semira had lived, but that didn't make any sense. Ultimately he just kept heading eastward, toward Cologne's medieval old town and the Rhine, which runs north-south through the middle of Cologne.

Martin was in high spirits like a kid on Christmas Eve. He was driving frenetically, blathering on about all kinds of nonsense without stopping to take a breath and sniffling about seventeen times. But he didn't have a runny nose. Just nerves. It was driving me crazy. I hate it when people sniffle. I know, my manners weren't always the best, either, but I always kept my nose clean—that is a minimum standard of civilization that I retained throughout my whole life. I asked Martin to stop. He said, "Yes, of course," and then he sniffled again. He didn't even notice. I suppressed my disgust and left him alone so I wouldn't make him even more nervous. After all, he had to keep track of the Jag, keep an eye on the road, watch out for traffic, and stop at red lights, even if the Jag darted through a yellow. But we always caught up with him again at the next light; that's the benefit I guess to a totally uncoordinated traffic light system.

Our drive took us across the Rhine, the cathedral receding downriver behind us to the left, and Martin got even more nervous as he considered the possibility that we might soon be running on empty, but it didn't come to that. The Jaguar turned off the main road.

"Industrial wasteland" is a buzzword that describes a piece of land where some kind of industrial operation used to be located. First the operation brings in wads of cash while regrettably contaminating the soil and groundwater, then it's closed, falls into disrepair if the site wasn't in ruins already, and then the former owner or heirs no longer can or want to be found—thereby sticking the general public with the costs of decontaminating the poison pit. That's the kind of site our stylin' Jaguar was driving to.

Martin turned on his blinker to follow, but before he could execute this hair-raisingly idiotic idea, I talked him out of it with a carefully worded question.

"Are you batshit crazy?" I roared.

Martin hit the brakes as hard as he could. Pure reflex.

"We're going to stick out like Santa Claus at Easter Sunday mass if we follow behind the Jag now," I said, returning to normal intonation.

"Right, got it," Martin moaned, sniffling.

"We're going to have to keep a low profile and follow him on foot," I said. "So park the car here, and let's get going."

Martin parked the trash can on the shoulder, awkwardly locked the doors, and started walking at a brisk pace.

To our benefit, all kinds of bushes and trees had already taken over the abandoned site as their habitat, so we didn't need to walk around without any cover. I whooshed out in front as a scout, found the Jag not far from us, and even caught another glimpse of Dr. Eilig, who was walking up to a dilapidated building, attaché case in hand. I was torn between going back to Martin and staying with Eilig, but I ultimately decided on Eilig. Presumably that was my error because Martin wasn't keeping an eye out behind him, either—only in front.

Dr. Eilig took up position on the front steps of the old building, its roof totally missing and its rear gable wall half caved-in, and then looked around. Obviously he couldn't see me, and he couldn't see Martin from his location, either. After looking all around again, Eilig stood there for a moment almost hesitantly, but finally he set the attaché case down in the entryway to the old building and walked at a rapid gait back to his Jaguar, climbed in, and drove off.

Martin had just enough time to dive behind a wall as the car raced past him. We couldn't tell if Eilig saw him.

A few seconds later Martin had reached the attaché, which I hadn't let out of my sight the whole time. "What's inside?" he asked.

"How am I supposed to know?" I asked.

"Can't you see inside it? Or seep into it, or something?" Martin demanded.

"And do you suppose there's a little light bulb inside, like in the fridge?" I asked back.

"Well I don't know," Martin mumbled.

"Why don't you just open it?" I suggested.

"And what if it's a bomb?" Martin asked.

"Is it ticking?" I asked.

Martin listened and shook his head.

"So open it," I said.

He lay the case down carefully, gently pressed on the locks, and the cover sprung open. No bomb. Money. Hundred-euro bills. More than I'd ever seen in one stack before. Sweet!

"Take the attaché and let's get out of here," I said. Martin stood there as though he were nailed to the spot.

"Martin!" I yelled, but he showed no reaction.

"He's being blackmailed," Martin mumbled thought-fully. "Eilig is being blackmailed."

"That's how I see it, too," I said. "And that means: we've got a problem. To be specific, the blackmailer is going to be showing up in a minute to pick up his cash. We need to clear out of here now."

"Why is he being blackmailed?" Martin mused to no one in particular.

"He's got a whole pile of skeletons in his closet," I said. "And you don't screw around with people like that. So hobblety-hobblety-ho, let's go."

Martin didn't move. "But who knows about the skeletons in his closet?"

Here again you can see how complicated these college-educated types make life. When confronted with a case full of money, what on earth does a normal person care who is blackmailing who? No one gives a fuck; the main thing is you get to get your hands on the dough. But not Martin.

Martin was taking his own sweet time thinking things through.

"Why did Eilig need to have killed you, actually?" he asked.

"Because I stole his car and knew that there was a body in it," I replied.

"But how did he know that you were the thief?"

"He must have seen me breaking into the car."

"What could he have seen?" asked Martin the Meticulous, who had never yet just believed the blatantly obvious.

I thought about it. Eilig could have seen only a thin, inconspicuous guy in dark clothes with a cap on driving away in his car. No one followed me as I drove the car to the rendezvous point. No one was standing in the parking lot when I handed the car off. Eilig had no way at all of knowing who I was. Therefore, he was not the one who killed me. But who was it then? And why was Eilig being blackmailed? I asked Martin this as well, since he had infected me with his brooding, and as a result I totally forgot about the danger we were in.

"Why he was being blackmailed is easy," Martin said. "Because of the body in the trunk."

"Makes sense," I said.

"The only question is: by whom?"

The answer hit us at the same time: I had gotten a job from someone to steal the SLR. That someone intended to sell the car in Eastern Europe and had almost certainly discovered the body in the trunk first. His contact in the East . . . At that moment everything became clear to me: his contact was a tall, thin, good-looking, dark-haired guy who I'd seen for the first time on the day I died, then in Olli's shop, and most recently at the Institute for Forensic Medicine. All the threads in this case converged into the fat hands of one man:

"Olli." I thought it to myself, but Martin yelled out the name loud and clear.

"That's right," said a completely calm voice that I immediately recognized as Olli's, from barely five meters away. "And that's why the money belongs to me and I will thank you to get your manicured hands off it right now."

Martin and I stood there as though flash-frozen. We hadn't heard Olli coming; he had just suddenly emerged from the semiruined building. Maybe he'd been hanging around there the whole time. I don't know; I hadn't noticed him.

"Uh-oh . . ." Martin said as he too recognized the obese car smuggler. The activity in his brain was sending out sparks.

"Of course," Martin said. "You had no need to find out whose SLR it was; you had already hired someone to steal a unique car."

Olli nodded.

"And when the car was delivered to you with a body in the trunk, the situation was just begging for blackmail," Martin said.

Olli nodded again. "I'd have been stupid not to ask for some cash on the side."

"But why did Pascha Lerchenberg have to die?" Martin asked.

Olli stopped short. "How do you get to him?"

"He's the one who stole the SLR," Martin said, as though it was the most natural thing in the world that Martin knew that.

Olli's eyes narrowed between the jiggling fat above and below them into even thinner slits.

"You're the guy who knew that I had your girlfriend's BMW," Olli said.

Martin nodded.

"And now you know that Pascha stole the SLR," Olli said.

"I already knew that before I stopped by your lot," Martin said, correcting him.

"And where do you know all of this from?" Olli asked.

Martin wrestled with himself. Should he tell him that he had contact with my immortal soul? He decided to tell the truth because he couldn't think of a suitable lie. That is pretty much the most dim-witted reason for telling the truth, but my own creativity was totally hamstrung by this special situation, so I couldn't blame him.

Olli reacted as expected. In an already-quivering voice he asked, "Is that really true? Like Patrick Swayze and Demi Moore in *Ghost*?"

Martin nodded.

And then the tears started flowing from Olli's eyes again, his double chin jiggled, and the entire man started losing it.

This was presumably our last chance!

"Take off," I urged Martin. "Fast, while he's still distracted."

Martin didn't want to. He wanted answers—all of them. He was acting as calmly and rationally as he does in his autopsy room, examining a body for as long as it takes to definitively find the cause of the death. He was welcome to do that normally, of course, but here his doggedness was inappropriate and imperiling his life. I begged and pleaded, for naught. He seemed unable to perceive me at all, he was so focused on solving the various deaths and blackmailings.

"You could have blackmailed Dr. Eilig without killing Pascha," Martin suggested.

"I did not murder that little shit," Olli sniffled, blowing his nose. He was pulling himself together. We missed our chance.

In view of this new information, Martin thought briefly but single-mindedly about the case, and then came to a realization: "Then Semira's brother killed Pascha?"

Olli grew pale as the wall. "You know her name?"

"Of course," Martin said. "Semira's brother actually came to the Institute to have her body transported back home. He had her papers with him."

"Semiiira," Olli wailed, and started weeping again.

Martin stared at him in disbelief, but then we both simultaneously remembered what Semira's neighbor had told us. She mentioned a man who came to visit Semira. A fat man with fat cars. Olli!

"You were Semira's pimp," Martin said.

Olli shook his head. "Agent," he mumbled.

"Did Semira's brother know how his sister was earning her money?" Martin asked.

"Of course not," Olli cried. "He would have killed her. And then me right afterward."

"How did her brother find out Semira was dead?" Martin asked.

Olli dropped back onto a ledge on the wall, drained and limp. "I obviously took a picture of the body in the trunk because I couldn't let Eilig get away with it," he began. "But Sjubek discovered the photo."

"And?" Martin asked.

"And, what? He obviously wanted revenge, to kill the guy who killed his sister," Olli said as though he kept having to explain to a child that you spread jam on your bread, not on your hands.

"And you of course didn't want Sjubek to kill Dr. Eilig," Martin said smugly.

Fortunately Olli didn't have a feel for such nuances at the moment, otherwise he'd probably have felt provoked. "Of course not," Olli said. "I wanted to blackmail the guy, right? And dead people don't pay. Make sense?"

Martin nodded. I could feel that Martin was starting to seriously doubt his own mental health. Here he was standing in an industrial wasteland across from a rotund car smuggler who was explaining to him how much sense it makes to prevent a murder—not for humanitarian reasons but to blackmail the potential murder victim. Martin was wondering who here was normal and who was nuts.

"I still don't understand why Pascha had to die," Martin said after he thought his way back to me.

"Sjubek was out of his mind. He had to avenge his sister's death, and he needed a scapegoat."

"But his sister actually died from an allergy to hazelnuts," Martin said.

"That doesn't matter now," Olli said dismissively. "Anyway, I put it into Sjubek's head that Pascha felt guilty about offing his sister. That's how I kept Sjubek busy: he got to act on his thoughts of vengeance, and Pascha couldn't get in my way anymore. I assumed Pascha knew there was a body in the trunk; he would have come up with the idea of blackmailing the guy as well."

"How convenient," Martin said. "Killing two pesky birds with one stone . . ."

"Shit," I said. "I would never have come up with the blackmailing idea, not even in my wildest dreams."

None of us said anything for a moment.

"And why did Sjubek have to die?" Martin asked.

"That idiot was making a big fuss because we let his sister's body go missing," Olli said. "He absolutely wanted to give her a proper funeral."

Martin nodded; even I could understand that. But not Olli, apparently.

"When the body turned up again, because that brain-dead Kevin just wrapped it and dumped it somewhere instead of burying it, Sjubek went to the cops so he could transport Semira back home, even though he didn't have proper immigration papers. He was even risking a visit to the pen and deportation just for Semira's funeral."

"And then at the Institute he found out his sister hadn't been killed after all?" Martin guessed.

Olli nodded. "He came to me and wanted an explanation."

"And then you killed him."

"Of course."

This was all very interesting, but in the meantime even our naïve little Martin had to have realized that he was standing opposite a man who had committed multiple murders, who was confessing all of his foul deeds down to the last detail—and that it was high time to end this amicable conversation and bail!

Happily, the same thought finally occurred to Martin. He took an awkward step backward.

"Just a moment," Olli said. "The attaché case."

Martin handed it to Olli, who took it with his left hand.

In a lightning-fast motion I wouldn't have thought him capable of, Olli suddenly shot his right arm forward. For a fraction of a second I could see the glint of the cold steel, then it sunk into Martin's duffle coat fairly accurately, right where his heart should have been.

Olli slowly shook his thick head. "I'm really sorry, man, but you know way too much."

Martin stared at fat Olli, surprised.

"I'm sorry about your girlfriend, too," Olli said. "But, you know. At least she got her BMW back." He sounded like he meant it.

Martin staggered, then he grabbed the left side of his chest and collapsed. I was speechless, aghast, horrified. Even I hadn't expected this. I'd never seen Olli with a weapon. Car smugglers are in principle friendlier sorts of criminals.

As though through a thick fog I could see Olli pick up the case with the money and turn to go. Then he stopped, slipped a thick signet ring with a striking black stone off his pinkie and stuck it into Martin's pants pocket, then disappeared through the derelict building he had just emerged from.

Martin stayed behind—in the middle of the night, in a shady location, with a flashy ring that didn't belong to him, and a life-threatening injury.

I hovered close over Martin, trying to get hold of his thoughts, and I found myself suddenly confronted with an incorporeal soul floating over Martin at the same altitude as I was. Martin!

"Hey, get out of here!" I yelled. "Get back into your body!"

"Oh, but it's so calm and peaceful here," Martin's ghost slowly said. "Down there is nothing but pain and suffering."

"Enough of this horseshit—go back!" I bellowed at him. "You can take that tiny bit of pain!"

As Olli disappeared with his cash and the sound of a fat engine revving up pealed through the abandoned site, Martin's soul and I furtively watched each other like two gamecocks, although I was the only one actually acting aggressively. Martin's soul was acting solemn and placid. I didn't know how this trial of strength would have turned out if at that very moment a voice hadn't bellowed out from a megaphone.

"You are surrounded, resistance is futile!"

Had those dopes been struck completely blind? I thought. There's a guy lying here in the mud slowly but surely bleeding to death, and these idiots are talking about resistance!

"He's dead," one of the policemen said as he approached, shooter drawn.

"He is not dead!" I roared as loud as I could. "Get the paramedics over here!"

They were already on the way, but those two minutes until they arrived felt like an eternity to me. They got a bag of blood set up and flowing into Martin right away, and I was able to talk his little soul into at least staying close by his body and not taking the direct route to heaven. The cops waited until Martin had been carried off, half-dead. Then the forensic squad arrived, and the whole shebang that would last for hours began.

From the various conversations among the police I learned that the cops had been sent to the site by a traumatized dog owner who, while out for a walk, had unwittingly been witness to a stabbing. Martin was taken under police escort with his life-threatening injury to the hospital where emergency surgery would hopefully avoid his delivery as a corpse to the morgue. A mysterious ring was in his pocket, which Olli had certainly not deposited there as a memento of a pleasant evening.

I came down on myself hard. I was the only reason that Martin had gotten stuck in this situation, and I was the only reason he had lost his girlfriend and his reputation—and maybe even his life. This couldn't be happening!

I couldn't do anything to save his life. And maybe I couldn't do anything about his girlfriend, either, but I could at least try to save his reputation. After all, apart from Martin I was the only good guy left who knew the whole story. And I had to tell the story somehow, because Martin couldn't talk, and even if he could no one would have believed him. The only question was to whom and how should I recount the events of the past two weeks. Except for Martin I still hadn't found anyone who could hear me. But I'd have to come up with something—that much was clear. I owed him that.

———•———

I zoomed faster than a jet back over to the Institute, because I was hoping people there had heard about the events and I could get some news. But it still took a few hours before Katrin came running distraught into the break room, yelling, "Martin was stabbed and is in surgery in critical condition! The police had him under surveillance."

Awesome, he wasn't dead yet—that was my first piece of good news all day. Katrin continued by saying they were currently looking for the man who had tried to kill him. Everyone was shocked. No one could imagine Martin being involved in any kind of crime. On the other hand, everyone at the Institute had noticed how weirdly he'd been acting the past few days. People had been doubting Martin's innocence more and more, but now suddenly people's suspicions also started sticking to him like dog shit to treaded soles. Martin couldn't defend himself. It made me sick.

I felt like being close to Martin again, so I slunk over to his desk, where I stared into space in gloom.

"Assholes," I mumbled.

The screen flickered on, and the word "assholes" appeared.

I couldn't believe it. One look confirmed my hope: before Martin left the office on forced leave, he had left his computer just as it was. With his dictation software ready to go and his cordless headset activated. Apparently no one had checked whether his power guzzler here had been turned off or was just on standby. Hallelujah!

I tried it again: ". . . are what you call everyone who doesn't believe Martin."

Now I had a plan. I floated in front of the screen, close enough to be able to read well, and I started dictating: "I hope you'll read this account from top to bottom . . ."

———•———

That was about twenty-four hours ago. I dictated for twenty hours, with little breaks here and there. Now I've been hanging around here for four hours hoping that someone would finally look at this screen. I cursed the way everyone's cubicles were organized, because Martin's desk was the last one back by the wall with a view out over the whole room, meaning that you could see his screen only if you were standing back by the wall.

In the meantime I've learned that Martin is alive and on the road to a full recovery. He's not allowed to have any visitors, and no one has any idea yet what kind of business he'd gotten mixed up with, but the signet ring that has since been identified as the property of the murdered Moldovan is casting an extremely negative light on him. There are rumors that an arrest warrant is about to be issued for Martin for the murder of Semira's brother.

The mood in the office is depressed, and so far everyone has stayed clear of Martin's desk. I can only hope that will change soon. I keep writing an extra sentence once in a while so that the power-saving mode doesn't turn off the screen, because otherwise no one will ever see what I've written here.

I'm slowly getting nervous. What if no one . . . Ooh, here comes someone, exactly the right person. Yes, yes! Come over this way! Farther, past the other desks, back here to the last desk, to Martin's desk, yes! And now look at the screen!

HELLO KATRIN!!!

ACKNOWLEDGMENTS

From a strictly chronological perspective my first word of thanks goes to my elementary school teacher Helene Grimm, who in 1977 wrote in my friendship book: *Übermut tut auch mal gut* ("It does you good to be cocky sometimes, too"). I've stuck to that advice ever since.

From a more current perspective my thanks must go to Dr. Frank Glenewinkel, my contact in the world of forensic medicine. He not only answered all my questions with patience, but—neither intentionally nor consciously—he also gave me the idea for this book. Anyone who gives a talk in front of a group of women authors simply has to be prepared for anything . . .

But the ultimate megathanks are due to my editor Karoline Adler, who for years has harbored an unshakable faith in our shared future. Without her I would never have made writing my profession and this book may never have come to be.

Jutta Profijt

ABOUT THE AUTHOR

© privat

Jutta Profijt was born in 1967 in Ratingen, Germany. After finishing school, she lived abroad working as an au pair, an importer/exporter, a coach to executives and students, and a business English instructor. She published her first novel in 2003 and today works as a free-lance writer and translator. Her first novel featuring coroner Martin Gänsewein, *Morgue Drawer Four,* was shortlisted for Germany's 2010 Friedrich Glauser Prize for best crime novel.

ABOUT THE TRANSLATOR

Erik J. Macki worked as a cherry-orchard tour guide, copy editor, Web developer, and German and French teacher before settling into his translation career—probably an inevitable choice, as he has collected foreign-language grammars, dictionaries, and language-learning books since childhood and to this day is not above diagramming sentences when duty so calls. A former resident of Cologne and Münster, Germany, and of Tours, France, he did his graduate work in Germanics and comparative syntax. He now translates books for adults and children as well as nonfiction material from his home in Seattle, where he lives with his family and their black Lab, Zephyr.